Praise For Where the Fireflies Dream

"Simple, heartwarming, painful, and lovely, all in perfect doses."

"This story captivates and keeps you spellbound from the start to the last page."

"Emily Nelson is a genius writer, using all the right words in all the right places."

"This book moved my heart on so many levels."

"So moving... amazingly descriptive... a fantastic first book."

"Wow! This story is so touching, sad, funny, sweet - it runs the gamut of emotions, but is above all very inspirational."

"An immense insight into the experience of grief."

"How can you describe a book such as this? It had me sobbing all the way through."

"A modern day To Kill A Mockingbird."

"Full of magnificent storytelling and prose."

"I haven't read many books that take you through so many emotions as this one does."

"A masterpiece of triumph."

"Your heart smiles and your heart cries... it's what every reader wants to experience."

"Very emotional and teary... I could not put it down."

"One of the most beautiful books I've ever read."

"This novel will break your heart and put it back together again."

"An emotion-filled page turner... so much pain, so much beauty..."

"This one is a real tear jerker! Get the tissues!"

"My favorite author... a must-read book."

"A moving testimony to human resilience."

"This author has a gift."

"Nelson really hits a home run on this novel."

"Beautifully written... I couldn't put it down!"

"Simply put: brilliant!"

"It will touch your heart so deeply, and have you crying before the end."

"One of the most heartwarming stories I've ever read."

"Such a heart-wrenching, heart-filling story."

"I literally read this book in a day and was ready to share it with everyone I knew!"

"There was a part of me that broke and healed at the same time... truly a must read in today's world."

"I loved it from the moment I started to read."

"This book beautifully words what I have been looking to understand."

Where the Fireflies Dream

A Novel

EMILY NELSON

EVERMORE PUBLISHING

Note From The Author

This novel is filled with deep hope, but also with truth that may be triggering for some. Sensitive topics, including various forms of abuse, are explored in depth. Please engage with caution.

May you find the same healing in these words that many other readers have expressed.

for the invisible ones

Prologue

33 Years Old

2020

Fireflies

When I was a child, I'd watch the fireflies on hot summer nights outside my windowsill and wonder in awe at what it'd be like to be that free, to float like magic to faraway places and glow.

I wanted to go to that place, where the fireflies dream, and stay forever, drifting into a world where the wind would carry me somewhere so gentle, so safe, I only needed soft wings.

I dreamed while awake of a world where I was *loved*.

Part One

8 Years Old

1995

Monster

I didn't want to open my eyes because I knew what reality held, what awaited me the very moment I did. If only God would give me five more minutes of peace... just five more. It was only four a.m., yet already, it had begun. I could feel the thunderous power in his gruff voice; hear the piercing impact of his slap. I knew the rage that was overflowing in his eyes; his balled-up, fist tight hands.

My mother whimpered in the distance quietly, but I had learned to pick up the sound of her small, shaken sobs, the ones she tried so unsuccessfully to hide. The birds were vocalizing their morning dawn chorus and gentle, rhythmic rain was falling in calming sheets; the day ahead would no doubt be beautiful. I was covered up with cozy, quilted blankets and plush teddy bears, yet underneath it all, I lay shivering uncontrollably, shaken and frozen in place though I wished so badly to run. I looked at the unforgiving, glowing digits of my clock again. It was 4:03 a.m.

I closed my eyes reflexively as a roaring thud echoed down the hall, shaking the floor violently in its wake. An ebb and flow of suffering was happening just beyond me, the screams were rising and falling again. My mother's noises were animal, base and shrill, as she cried and fought the monster. A vehement laugh expelled from his wicked lips at the sound of her body hitting the ground like a heavy log. I turned my head and covered my ears to block out the chaotic noise, yet it seemed to echo loudly more than ever before. I tried to sing the song I learned last week in Vacation Bible School, but I couldn't remember the words. For a brief moment, the crying stopped and I wondered if my mother was really dead this time. The threat of death always hung over this house like a cloak, covering us all in black darkness.

My body was shaking, but I kept singing, though the words ran together and were jumbled. My small, weak voice did not hold enough power to block out all that I was trying not to hear, but I pretended that it was. Suddenly, the house went strangely silent. As I pressed my ear against them, I could hear nothing through the cardboard-thin walls and I wondered if he was really gone. Then, in the sudden stillness, I heard a familiar, foreboding sound, one that scraped around my mind and made my stomach turn inside out: the brittle snap of the can opening and the foam fizzing as it seethed out. I hoped I was not right, though I knew with all certainty that I was.

As gently and as quietly as possible, I moved out of my bed, hiding the sound of my feet by using my tiptoes. In fear, I held my breath as I walked across the dingy carpet. Then I peered around the shadowed corner and found that all my nightmares were alive, flesh and blood: my father was sitting in his worn, grimy recliner, a can of beer upturned in his large hand. The foam fell freely down his rounded, robust chin and as he reached up aimlessly to wipe it, the channel flipped to one I had never seen before. There were pretty women without any clothes on, and I was scared without knowing why. It made me feel so ashamed and embarrassed in the deep down corners of my heart. I stared at the empty, unvacuumed floor for a long time and then back up at my father, hoping against expectation that he had stopped. He hadn't; I watched his evil sneer as he relished the screen of unreal women. I had never seen anything so despicable, not even from him. I grabbed my mouth with both hands and fell against the nearby wall. I could feel the chunks of bile rising in my throat.

I heard a snarled sound coming from the ground and looked toward it. In the darkness, I had to squint carefully just to see. Even then, it was only by the faint, flashing light of the TV that I could see my mother's outline, grabbing her stomach and throwing up blood, as she weakly crawled across the floor with her one barely useable arm. I longed to run to my mother, to help her up, to comfort her, to be her arms, and I started to, only to realize that I couldn't move. Fear had glued my feet squarely in place. I knew I would never be able to forget the way she looked, her battered, thin frame broken in pieces, her naturally gorgeous, bronze face busted open like dropped, fragile glass. I felt like a coward, maybe even as bad as him. The sensation hung over me like a thunderstorm, threatening and sudden. I couldn't stand it any longer; I looked away.

I tiptoed back down the hall, holding my breath, hoping he wouldn't see me in the dim light. My heart was broken, in every way, and I felt my throat begin to tighten in on itself. I threw up everywhere, in uncontrollable chunks and bouts of rousing nausea. My balance wavered and I fell into the dusty vacuum in the hallway, knocking it over with a deafening crash. My father pounced from his chair and searched the hallway diligently, his drunken steps unstable and invasive. I looked for a realm of safety deep in the obscurity of the walls, trying so hard to stop quivering, but the unmatched fear was too much. He heard it: my throat making noise as I continued to throw up wildly, though I had tried so hard to hold it in.

He saw my tiny body crumpled in the corner and began moving towards me with the steps of a giant. I felt the walls shaking thunderously as he stalked toward me and reached down angrily to take hold of my frayed nightgown. Suddenly, his large shadow fell with a deep, resounding thud, a giant slain. He had fallen right in front of me, a passed out drunk, my pink nightshirt still clutched in his mighty grasp.

I finally yanked my clothes out of his hot, greasy hands and stepped over him quickly, not looking at his ghostly white face. I was too scared to try, afraid that I might see his dead green eyes staring back at me, cutting me like a knife to my very bone. I solemnly walked to the blaring TV, glancing behind me at his unmovable frame the entire time, praying he wouldn't move. I could not watch what was on the screen and the sound alone made my stomach rumble with disgust. I hit the power button as hard as I could and all was forgivingly quiet. In the darkness, I reached out along the textured walls, feeling the pin-prick of their edges, until I made it into the back corners of my bedroom.

My breathing was coming out in spurts: shallow and uneven. I covered my mouth with my hands, afraid that the noise would wake the snoring monster and make him come after me again. I climbed into my closet and set aside the cubbies that held my toys, moving the broken piece on the left and climbing inside the wall, into my secret hideaway, the piece closing again behind me. Then, for the first time in days, I breathed without worrying, knowing he couldn't hear me. I began to cry, the moment overwhelming my young soul, and tried desperately to scream, but my mind wouldn't let me.

I held Wammie, my favorite baby doll, and whispered to her that it was okay. I knew she was scared, too. I opened the secret hole, grabbed a tiny brush, and began to fix my doll's knotted hair. My breathing finally slowed and I remembered the words to the song that I learned at Vacation Bible School. *'Jesus loves me, this I know, for* the Bible tells me so, little ones to Him belong, they are weak, but He is strong, Yes, Jesus loves me, Yes, Jesus loves me.' I stayed with Wammie, brushing her hair, for a long time, hoping she wasn't scared, too. I kissed her forehead and told her that she was my friend. I sang the song I learned to her, but made it say 'Yes, Jesus loves Wammie' instead of 'me'.

Finally, I left the safe refuge of my closet, ever so quietly. I put my shuffled cubbies back in their usual places, but brought sweet Wammie with me. There was no way I could ever leave her behind, my only friend in the world. I cracked the squeaky bedroom door open slightly, just enough to see the drunken monster in the pale morning light, still keeled over on the floor, lifeless and sweaty. Disgusted and relieved, I closed the door, locking it tightly and pulling on the handle again and again, just to be sure it was locked.

Feeling spent, I collapsed into my bed wearily, filled with fluffy stuffed animals, and kissed them all goodnight one by one, my perfect little treasures. I snuggled in deep, turning my head to view the glowing digits of the clock; it was now 5:19 a.m., Monday. I tossed and turned for hours that seemed like days, but soon gave up. I knew it was pointless to even try. Underneath my warm, inviting covers, my entire little body was trembling, as if I'd seen a monster. Maybe I had, the fear of his sandpaper hands and bourbon musk as close to me now as my ragged, held breath.

The Freckled Faced Redhead

The beating rays of sunshine blazing down through my sheer curtains woke me later that day. I was groggy and listless, my weighted limbs as hard to move as bundles of heavy lumber. I didn't know how long I had been sleeping, but I knew it must have been at least a few hours because the sun had taken its place in the early morning sky; the birds were chirping and resuming their daybreak songs. I could feel the pure warmth of the sun as it found gentle rest on my skin, reviving me from the outside in.

I longed endlessly to leave my room, but was paralyzed with fear; it was a wall of protection and a suffocating prison in the exact same moment. I could feel the pressure laying on my heavy bladder like a weight, unsure how much longer I could restrain myself. Distantly, from the other room, I heard the muffled sound of my mother's voice begin speaking. I pressed my ear against the door to hear what was happening, pushing and straining until it was physically sore.

"I'm sorry," she apologized weakly, her words sounding small and fragile. "I'm so stupid. I should have never made you mad." My breath was in my throat as I opened the door, putting my hand on the knob and turning it without a single sound. She was crouching beside the monster, sitting at his feet, begging forgiveness, as he watched his filthy women on the muted screen. "I'll always love you," she cooed. "I'll do better, I will." My father sat unresponsively, no emotion on his face, ignoring her presence altogether. Finally, he pointed lazily, eyes still glued to the screen, in the general direction of the kitchen. "Get me a beer," he grunted demeaningly, only acknowledging her as his servant. I watched my mother carefully; she frantically bounded off the ground and rushed into the kitchen, half-tripping over herself in her hurry, a mess of flailing legs and a wrinkled satin nightgown. The volume on the TV reached deafening, piercing heights.

I stared down the hall towards the bathroom, only inches away from me now. I take a tentative step towards it, before thinking better and pivoting, returning to my lonely bedroom, the crushed, invisible girl. I didn't want to hear any more and I closed the door silently, safely imprisoned again. I let my body slide down the back of it, a loud thump resounding as I hit the floor. For the first time that I could remember, I didn't worry. I closed my eyes and fought back mountains of tears. I knew that he couldn't hear me.

I sat silently for a few minutes, listening to the sound of my heartbeat pounding loudly in my ears, hammering the agony into my very soul. Then, I began to pray, something that I had never done before; something I wasn't quite sure how to do at all. "Dear God," I muttered aimlessly, "Are you there? I don't know if you can hear me or not, the monster is being so loud, but I need to ask you a favor. I want a friend. Please. I just want someone who will love me, just a little bit. But if I can't have that, then I'm begging You, just let me meet someone who won't hurt me…"

My heart was still speaking, still crying out to a God that I wasn't sure was listening, but my prayer was forced to end there as my words were washed away and my voice lost strength completely beneath my cries. Just then, a loud, familiar moan came from the TV, and I could barely make out the sound of my mother saying, "Here, honey." I knew she had handed him the intoxicating beer and I felt my body begin to shake in expectation. It was only a matter of minutes before the cycle of abuse started up and I instantly ran to hide.

I hid away in the shadows of the darkness, those foreboding corners the light had yet to touch, and covered my ears with my hands, muffling the sounds of the devil, my mother's screams only vaguely audible. I could not hold it in anymore, the persistent, human urgency hitting me like a tidal wave, and I wet myself in fear. The sensation clung to my legs in sticky patches, like the time I spilt my mom's coffee and promptly was rewarded with a beating. My sheets were darkly spotted, completely ruined, the repugnant smell making me spontaneously vomit all over myself. I began to cry shamefully and tried to clean up the mess with one of my doll's prized dresses. I feared what would happen when he found out, the seizing, painful blows, and I began to shake fitfully again. I held Wammie, thankful the acrid smell had missed her, and made a makeshift pallet on the floor to lie on, the terror still hammering my mind. "I'm sorry," my little voice whispered, though I didn't know who I was talking to. A scream echoed outside my door and I heard the sound of shattering glass. My sorrowful eyes were wide and wracked with animal-like fear. "I didn't mean to do it."

A few day-long hours passed and finally, mama peeked her head slightly inside my door, barking orders fiercely at me. "Get ready for school," she demanded gruffly and I saw she was cradling a soaking wet rag against her wounded scalp, letting the blood-red fluid drip from her face onto it. She was angry, broken, disconnected in every way, and before I could say anything, she had closed the door with a slam once again.

Several days ago, I was told in no uncertain terms what to expect today. I would be walking to my first day of school with our neighbor, Jessica, and I was to keep my dirty mouth shut if I knew what was good for me. I hadn't met her yet and the anxiety I felt at the thought overwhelmed me completely. I didn't want to go to school at all; I wanted to remain small, blurry, edging quietly in the background of life, unnoticed. I knew if I was visible they would make fun of me. It wasn't a question. Of course they would. Everyone who noticed me always had.

I entered my doorless closet, standing on the dirty floor, covered in strings and pieces of lint, and looked for something pretty, or at least clean, that I could wear. Staring back at me were empty, half-broken hangers that hung lopsidedly like a bunny's ear. A mound of filthy, unkempt clothes in outgrown sizes laid beside me on the carpet. As I accepted my reality, I was so painfully embarrassed, to the bone. I knew all the clothes would all smell like urine after what I had done. The whole room reeked and the passing hours had only increased the stench. Quickly, I went through the jumbled pyramid, trying to find the least disheveled and wrinkled items, and put them on.

As I looked in the mirror, I felt blazingly ashamed, red-faced and on fire with disgrace. My hair was going in a million crazy directions, parts hanging loosely in my eyes, a huge piece towards the back cow-licked and uncooperative, all of it holding massive, unforgiving amounts of static. I knew I looked dreadful and smelled like a dumpster, but there wasn't one second to fix it. "Julia, hurry up!" I heard mama scream loudly from the living room. "Jessica is outside waiting! Can't you just do something right for once?"

I didn't have the heart to respond. Instead, I smoothed my wrinkled khaki colored shorts and threw on a T-shirt, hoping it was long enough to cover all the gooey, dried-on stains. I looked at my reflection to see a sad, scared little girl looking back. I sighed from somewhere deep inside my soul, deciding from that moment on I would never look in a mirror again. I quickly flew through the living room, reaching top speeds, avoiding the words my mother was spouting out, and onto the porch. I saw a little girl with flaming red hair staring at me, her freckled face looking like a fresh strawberry patch in the bright sunlight. She immediately ran up to me at full force, smiling as if she was tickled to see me.

"Hi Julia!" she giggled, though I just stared back blankly, a comical grimace frozen on my face. "My mama told me all about you," she said in her thick Southern twang, looping her arm in mine as we exited my gravel drive. She began to pull me along the sidewalk, her unwilling victim.

"I just know we will be great friends soon," she declared overconfidently, immobilizing my ability to respond once again. I eagerly tried to smile politely, not really knowing what else to do, thinking this girl just might be flat crazy. I knew I had to say something as she stared at me expectantly.

Her brightly colored Ariel shirt, from The Little Mermaid, was impossible to miss, so I told her it was pretty. It was. It was a lovely shade of pink, too, which I also told her that I liked, even though it made her flaming red hair stick out more. "Thanks," she said easily, loudly smacking her Bubbilicious gum with a big pop. She took out a new wad and offered it to me, obviously prepared for a shortage at any moment. "Want some?" she asked, eyebrows wagging, her gapy grin revealing she had lost her front two teeth very recently. I couldn't help it; I giggled. I took some, thinking it might serve as breakfast for my rumbling stomach. "Sure," I said, chuckling, feeling that I already liked her so much even though I had tried so hard not to.

When we walked inside our third-grade classroom, I saw an aged, grumpy woman staring, her darting eyes piercing us like arrows, the smoke trailing in wisps out of her ears. "Ladies," she said wrathfully, her black bouffant hair with touches of silver at the temples never moving. "Take your seats. Now," she demanded, the huge yardstick in her hand slapping against two empty desks authoritatively. This, *exactly this*, I thought with confirmed dread, was what I knew would happen here. She circled us like prey as the other children stifled their laughter, as giddy as they could be that it was aimed at anyone but them. Oh, what I'd give to be invisible again. "Late on the first day, are we, *hmm*?" She held the "hmm" out so long it sounded like our A/C unit right before it broke all of a sudden last summer, tired and struggling, dripping with drawn-out noise and condensation. Wildly, she slapped the yardstick against our desks again, making us both jump as they loudly reverberated under her strength.

"Well, this is *my* classroom, and in *my* classroom, no one is late. Do you understand?" she asked, her face drawing so close to ours that her beady green eyes stuck out like one of the big jewels on the Pretty Pretty Princess crown. I remembered the hours I'd spent longing for one, poring over the JCPenney catalog. I sat there staring at her with blank eyes, afraid to even nod, to even breathe. Jessica whimpered out an "uh huh" and the old woman backed away with her body still facing us, still staring us down, but apparently satisfied for the moment. "Now class," she said much-too-pleasantly, suddenly cheery out of nowhere, "like I was saying, I am Mrs. Kellerman." I looked at her uneasily, that frozen mound of unmoving hair mesmerizing me. This woman was shifty as far as I was concerned, her moods as unstable as a hanging bridge in a hurricane. I already didn't trust her. She turned around with slow, arthritic movements, facing the board, writing her name in perfectly practiced, cursive scrawl, but even the letters looked threatening as I sat there, stewing. She faced the class again and pointed to herself with that dumb, pointless yardstick, "And this," she said, her tone changing cold and coarse again, the bridge flailing in the storm, "is my classroom." Her condescending gaze rested on Jessica and me, the two thorns in her ample flesh.

The hours until our lunch break, undoubtedly a million, seemed to drag by, but finally the bell rang shrilly and we all scurried out like mice with fresh cheese to sweet freedom. I didn't have a lunch, no one had packed one for me, I realized in sudden panic, but Jessica told me not to worry. "My mom packed extra," she said generously, her sweet toothy grin flashing my way. "Okay," I said, immensely relieved, but too shy to show it.

I sat with Jessica and two other black-haired girls who were sisters at lunch, Anna and Candace. They had just moved to town all the way from Oregon and they talked funny, not like me. "On the other side of the U.S., you mean?" I asked, astonished, and they both nodded proudly. I had never, ever known anyone from that far away before. It seemed like a different world to me. Besides my parents and Jessica, I really didn't know much of anyone. I was shocked to realize it; guess I'd never really thought much about it before. After finishing up lunch, it was time for recess and like freed prisoners we couldn't get outside fast enough.

Jessica and I were running so fervently to the iron hanging swings we accidentally ran smack dab into one of three little blonde girls. They were triplets and strikingly beautiful, so beautiful that I wanted to be just like them, all tumbling, lush, soft golden hair and piercing cobalt blue eyes. "Hi," I said nervously, initiating a conversation for the first time ever. I smiled broadly, anxiously awaiting a response at any moment, my young heart expectant and exuberant.

They smirked at one another and laughed with delight as they looked at me, their inferior, with contempt. "What," the littlest one of them asked mockingly, "You think we're going to talk to *you*?" The comment struck me like lightning, the color draining rapidly from my already pale face as the wind suddenly gusted and began to pick up. The smell of urine wafted from my clothes, leaving a stench-filled, gagging aroma in its trail.

"Ahhh," they screamed, wrenching in horror while covering their noses. Apparently, they could smell me, too. I walked away, their crushing blow draining my strength, and sat down on the nearest abandoned swing, without a soul in sight. I didn't want anyone else to smell me and cover their nose, too. Jessica walked over casually and sat beside me, ignoring the tornado of activity around us. "You don't have to..." I began, mortified she was standing so close, trying to imagine what I smelled like to her. She looked at me with kindness, her spirit washing over my rolling tears, warm and inviting. "Don't have to what Julia?" she asked grinning broadly, "I love to swing."

A few minutes later the blonde triplets began stomping resolutely toward us again, instantly invoking my fear and panic. Realizing what was happening, Jessica quickly sprung off her swing midair and began to hurry across the playground, the soles of her already dusty bare feet now coal-black. "Come on," she instructed hurriedly, rushing me further, "let's go play jump rope... now." I silently skulked in the direction she was headed, peering behind me as I tried to keep up. I was the prey once again, unskillfully dodging the pursuits of my predators. I viewed the triplets coming our way and cringed as they began to surround me. The folds of my heart seemed to collapse on one another, each one giving way to the next. I just wanted them to leave me alone, to take their sabotage anywhere but here, this place where my shaky hands and smelly clothes lived.

Jessica attempted to ignore their presence and pulled out a lengthy jump rope, rapidly unwinding the toy. She saw another young girl sitting nervously by herself, her bouncy strawberry-blonde curls twirling between her fingers aimlessly, and invited her to play with us. "You go first, Julia," they encouraged gently and I did. I trustingly stepped in between them and began jumping to the steady beat, following their lead and learning as I went along. My feet pounded in repeated rhythm on the pavement and I was instantly enraptured, my smile graciously beaming from ear to ear.

Then, suddenly, I heard the chanting begin behind me, and like a sharp knife cutting the air, my world instantly divided, the incision slicing my heart and wiping my smile away completely. "Julia is jumping rope, come now and see, she is S-M-E-LL-I-N-G!" The blonde girls forcefully stopped the jump rope and I turned around to face them, and though I searched so hard, I couldn't find a single thing to say. Our entire classroom had gathered around me and were laughing, pointing and jeering, with the exception of Jessica, the sisters from Oregon, and one little boy with dark eyes whose name I didn't know. I looked around aimlessly for help from Mrs. Kellerman, a defeated, last ditch effort, but she was still in the classroom, cellphone glued to her ear, absolutely nowhere to be found.

When we returned inside after recess, our teacher noticed that some of us were scratching our heads, clawing and scraping vigorously at the itchy spots. Repulsed at the very sight, she sent us to see the school nurse promptly, wanting us gone as quickly as possible. Jessica and I were among them and we scratched so hard that there was blood on our fingernails when we pulled our hands away. The nurse confirmed we all had lice, tracing it back to a shared hairbrush most likely, one thing I quite obviously did not have. Even so, most of the kids blamed me for the outbreak anyway. In a way I understood. I was just *so dirty*.

By the time we left the nurse's office, it was the end of the day and I was flooded with relief that it was time to walk home with Jessica again, the one person I actually liked who liked me. It had been an unbearably long day. We grabbed our belongings hastily and left the building in a rush. Even though I *knew* I didn't own a hairbrush, that it couldn't *possibly* be my fault in the least, as I watched the hard stares of my classmates, I somehow felt that it was.

"Jullliia," Jessica said, bringing me back in a sudden flash from my contemplation. "Did you like school?" she pried hopefully, her Bubbilicious gum sticking out slightly through her gaped, open teeth. I smiled at her appreciatively, thinking she was the nicest person that I had ever met. "Parts," I said as we walked down the sidewalk, taking in the fresh late summer day, the sunshine warming me to my very core. "You are really nice. I'm glad that I get to walk with you."

"Me too!" she said excitedly, smacking her gum again, relishing the flavor. "You know," she said as though she were trying to enlighten me, "You are the only person I know who doesn't make fun of my freckles." I was surprised when she said this, surprised that anyone could ever make fun of a girl like her.

"Make fun of them?" I scoffed, taken aback at the thought, looking at their sprinkled pattern. "I love them. They're like little strawberries all over your face."

She giggled self-consciously, covering her rose-petaled mouth. "Hey, I think I like that," she said genuinely. We walked along a little further down the sidewalk before she spoke again.

"Can I ask you something, Julia?" she wondered aloud, her voice growing unexpectedly grim.

"Yeah," I mumbled, my breath strangely caught in my throat.

She stopped walking and looked at the pavement, her unwilling reluctance to speak frightening me. "It's just... what happened to your arms?" she asked, glancing at them vaguely, obviously trying not to look.

At her words, I harshly pulled my sleeves down and covered the blackened bruises that trailed up my body with my shirt. I felt as though she'd looked right into my soul, as if all my secrets were laid bare with one glance from her eyes. I hesitated for a moment and then, at the memory of her inviting spirit, I relented.

"Sometimes my daddy... well, sometimes I make him really mad and he yells... and, and," I stuttered. "And he hits me... but, but it's an accident." I mumbled clumsily, trying to draw a veil over the truth.

Her light eyes stared at me with worry, piercing like a sword through my brave front. "Are you okay?" she asked quietly, not wanting to shame me.

"He doesn't mean to get so mad," I said, cowardly dodging the question, wondering why I was defending a man who beat me senselessly. It'd been only hours since the small places between my ribs felt like they were closing in and I'd absolutely die if I tried to breathe too hard. Inside me, I could sense the fear reaching a new pinnacle, ready to explode. I tried not to think about that anymore.

We reached her massive, gated house and she stopped short. "One second," she said, running inside without explanation. Moments later, she burst out again, emerging with a new, crisp pair of white shorts. "I think we are about the same size," she said proudly, her voice as beautiful to my ears as lilies in springtime. "Here."

I looked at them and felt my chin begin to shake. They were brand new, clean, designer shorts, ones that I had seen in catalogs and on the rich girls, but never could dream of having, of holding in my unwashed hands. I held them limply, afraid they could never really be mine. "I can't take these," I told her brokenly, grateful and unworthy in one breath.

She gracefully pushed them into my hands and enclosed my grasp around them. "Just say thank you," she told me sweetly, and I did just that.

"Meet me here tomorrow, okay? Same time?"

I nodded yes, the lump in my throat preventing me from speaking. "K, bye, Julia!" she said, unaware that she had just changed my life, rushing back towards her front door as if it were just another day.

"Oh," she said, spinning back around and heading towards me once again, as if she'd absentmindedly forgotten something. I anxiously began to wonder if she had changed her mind about the shorts and I pressed them to my chest, hugging them goodbye, just in case. Seconds later, she was at my side again, wrapping me fervently in a hug, and as I tightly hugged her back, I suddenly felt like I was best friends with Strawberry Shortcake, beautiful sprinkled freckles and all.

Jungle Gym

Jessica's stick-straight, bright red hair caught my eye as she hurriedly bounded out of her sprawling double front doors. She had a new plastic blue headband in her hair that matched her outfit perfectly.

"Julia!" she called out with a friendly smile, "You're already here!"

"Yeah," I smiled shyly without showing my teeth, my cheeks puffing up at the movement. "Is it too early?"

"No! It's perfect," she said breathlessly, sprinting down her front porch steps and squeezing me in a hug. Her light, airy smell enveloped me, conjuring up an image of a field of faraway flowers.

"I love those shorts that I gave you! They look great. Do you like them?"

I smoothed down my white denim shorts with pride, feeling grown-up and wondrous. They were the only new pair that I had ever had and already they'd conformed to my body like they were tailored for it.

"I love them." Jessica smiled, her kind, calming presence drawing me in. "Great! Then let's go!"

She met me where I stood on the sidewalk and we began to walk together, our loudly beating hearts almost musical as we pounded the pavement in rhythm. "So what did the nurse say yesterday? You never told me... you know, about the lice."

I spoke small, careful words, afraid of her reaction. "I have them. I told my mom, but she said she wouldn't get them out. She told me that they would go away on their own."

"Ew!" Jessica's face contorted, waves of emotion flooding her face. "I had them too, but my mom got all of mine out last night. She washed all of our sheets and everything."

"Oh," I said, feeling rejected, wishing I had a mom like Jessica's, wondering how to wash those sheets myself. I paused for what seemed like forever. "Do you think that I'm gross?" I willed the words out of my mouth, not able to hold them in any longer.

She stopped walking mid-pavement and faced me, her hazel eyes the color of a cotton branch in the early half-light. "No," she said, her eyebrows deeply furrowed, looking remarkably offended I would even ask such a thing. "Why would you think that?"

My head itched as though I had a wicked case of poison ivy and I scratched at it openly like the backwoods country girl I once was. "I don't know," I mumbled glumly, my eyes keenly tracing the ground. "Because I don't have nice clothes or hair like you do, like all the girls in our class do." I bit my lip and waited to lose the only real friend I had ever known.

Jessica looked at me with her typical warm-hearted understanding. "Julia, I like you. We both love Disney princesses and the color pink. You sit with me at lunch and play jump rope with me at recess. You don't even make fun of my freckles when they stick out because of the sunlight."

I giggled, my deep coral cheeks blushing. Her freckles did stick out.

She continued on, "You're my friend, my best friend, and best friends don't like you for your hair. I just like you for you."

I now had growing tears in my autumn-colored eyes, but tried to pretend that I didn't.

"Thanks Jess," I whispered, looking up at the sky, trying not to blink and send the tears rolling down my face. "You're my best friend too."

With that, she smiled excitedly and took my petite hand in hers and we walked the rest of the way to school just like that. My head kept itching like crazy, but there was no way that I was ever going to let go to scratch it.

Mrs. Kellerman's cell phone rang loudly as she waved us out of the classroom quickly, listening with intrigue to whoever was on the other end, and laughing. "Recess time," she mumbled aimlessly as she hastily responded to her caller. "Oh, you won't believe the kids I got this year. I really don't get paid enough to deal with this after all this time. This one is so disgustingly dirty. Yeah, I'll send you a pic... You'd think the parents would be embarrassed to send her up here looking like that." I tried to hear and not hear at the exact same time and eventually her voice trailed off. Pushing it away, I focused on the excitement of the swing set. Jessica and I ran out the doors that led to the school's playground, squealing in unmatched delight.

"Nice shorts, Julia." I stopped just short of the swings and turned around to see the three little blonde girls from yesterday staring at me coldly. I could feel their disdain almost physically seeping into me. I faced their rude gaze and smoothed down my shorts self-consciously. "Thank you," I asserted, trying to muster the courage to look them in the eyes and treat them the way I longed to be treated. "I like your pink barrette."

The littlest one of the three stepped forward. She was so much smaller than me it was almost comical. I stood silently as she examined me from head to toe with undisguised disgust on her face. "So, where did you get them?" she questioned knowingly, smirking at my poor lot in life. "It's not like your daddy can afford them." The words split my soul and I stumbled for a response, looking at the girls blankly, noticing their matching new Calvin Klein shorts— all perfect, clean, and expensive, one of their endless dispensable pairs.

Jessica stepped forward and stood in front of me protectively. "I gave them to her. No one cares that your dad is the president of some stupid bank, okay? Just leave us alone." The blonde girls looked at one another amused and rolled their eyes, disgruntled at her comment. "Jessica," they said pointedly, "Your daddy is rich, too. You don't have to hang out with this loser. We know you feel *sorry* for her and all because she's so *dirty* and has *lice*, but it doesn't mean you have to be her friend."

I felt frozen in place as they openly laughed at me, the same way I did when the monster would beat me. I wanted to run, but my legs wouldn't let me. I hung my head sadly, my pounding heart squeezing my chest so hard I thought it'd burst. I didn't have the strength to fight them anymore. The Hampton girls looked down in revulsion as though they might vomit as I scratched my itchy head again.

I couldn't help but wonder what Jessica was thinking, if she was scared or afraid or angry or worst of all, if deep down she agreed with them completely. She stepped back from the arrogant, snooty girls and stood firmly by my side again, the decision already made. "Julia is my best friend. She will *always* be my best friend."

She reached for my hand as we began to walk away and then

paused, turning her full attention back to the triplets. "It's you three that I feel sorry for... you have everything in the whole world, but you still don't know how to be kind." Scarlett, Sicily, and Savannah Hampton gawked in surprise, their perfect-shaped mouths and Barbie Doll-like blue eyes opened extra wide. I don't think anyone had ever talked to them that way before, and they simply didn't know what to do.

We left them standing there, their mouths still agape, and ran to the swing set with renewed vigor. I pushed off the dusty ground with my feet, the gentle wind blowing through my hair, the cool breeze on my back as if for the first time. As I swung, I felt confident that I soared higher that day than ever before, a baby bird now taking her first flight.

When we were finished on the squeaky swing set, I ran joyously over to the jungle gym. "Race you to the top!" I shouted hurriedly to Jessica and began to reach for the first rung. Just before I could begin what seemed like my great ascent of Everest, I saw Steven, KJ, and Dawson jumping from the peak of the jungle gym all the way to the ground with purposeful might. Dawson landed right beside me on the ground, plopping down forcefully in the thick, watery mud, splashing a huge, treacherous puddle all over my new white shorts.

"Oh no!" I screamed in unbelieving horror, frantically trying to wipe the mud stains off. I saw Jessica's face wince slightly and knew that her shorts were completely ruined.

"You stupid, stupid boy!" I exclaimed as I tackled Dawson with everything I had, beating on his chest with my fist, sitting on top of him as I pounded again and again with sheer force.

"Julia, stop!" he yelled loudly while trying unsuccessfully to push me off of him. I barely even heard his voice, the fury racing through my veins and pulsing in my angry heart before flowing from my fists. "I hate boys!" I yelled as I pummeled him with even greater force, throwing globs of mud at his half-hidden face. "I hate you all!

You ruin everything! *Everything!*" Dawson finally began to fight back with more than words. "Julia, get off of me!" he screamed, defending himself, as he started punching me in the eye with all of his strength.

"Stop it, Dawson! Stop it!" Jessica was screaming loudly as she wildly ran towards the jungle gym, waving her arms in the air to garner his attention. "She gets enough of that at home!"

Dawson immediately stopped punching me and I grabbed my right eye in pain. The blood smeared onto my hand and it dripped down onto my new shorts, leaving thick, wet stains.

Jessica ran to save me and pushed Dawson away, with more force than I ever knew she had. "I told you to stop," she said, anger flaring in her sobering eyes. "She doesn't need anyone else to hurt her," she whispered as she tried to clean the blood from my eye with her shirt. "Don't worry Julia," she assured me, noting the blood as it dripped down and mixed with the mud all over my new shorts. She attempted weakly to smile. "I have another pair for you at my house."

Suddenly, a loud, scattered noise came from the other side of the jungle gym and I looked up to see the three little blonde girls staring at me with wet, crumpled eyes of understanding. They too now had stains on their new shorts.

Then the littlest one of them all came over and slowly extended her tiny, doll-like hand. She offered me the pink barrette, the bulging tears in her eyes now barely held at bay. I shook my head yes and she was intensely careful, taking her time as she took it out of her own bangs and placed it so gently in my unwashed, lice-filled hair. Then, in the middle of a bloodied, jungle gym fight, there were four little girls crying while the rest of the class looked on in total silence.

Black Eyes & Rocking Chairs

My walk home from school today was especially unbearable and long, the minutes dragging by like an unwanted winter. What normally took me ten minutes now took close to twenty-five, over double my usual time. It was purposeful. I was pulling my heavy feet along as slowly as I possibly could, my shoes scraping along the concrete and producing a *skid* sound I quite enjoyed. It was irritating, but for some reason I found it entertaining today, a welcome distraction of sorts.

Most of all, I was avoiding the soul-splitting trouble I would no doubt be in as soon as the monster laid his murderous eyes on me. I shivered profusely at the thought, and again, instinctively, my pace slowed to a snail's crawl. A light, frigid drizzle began to fall and I pulled closer my pink, short-sleeved shirt, trying to stretch the cotton material to better cover my damp, cold arms. Frustrated and angry, I wished again that I had a jacket to wear, or even a stupid, ugly poncho like the girls whose mom drove the gold minivan, the one with the "Warning: Mama Bear On Board" bumper sticker on the back. So *dumb*.

Jessica had already gone home for the day, so I was stuck walking alone. Her mom, her uptight, annoying mom with her color-coordinated charts and weekly growth goals, came in to help with a class project earlier this afternoon. When she heard what happened with Dawson, she told Jessica there was no choice but to ride home with her. The BMW awaited. Her mom didn't like me very much, but I hoped she would change her mind in time because Jessica was my absolute best friend, the very best part of my often-grey world. The perfectionist wouldn't even let her talk to me before I left, distracted and busy with charts and graphs again. I saw Mrs. Kellerman rolling her eyes when she looked away for a moment and was surprised; could've sworn those two would be bosom buddies.

Yet still, in the weathered left corner of my backpack, my faithful note, like I had hoped, was waiting expectantly. It was on a pink sheet of construction paper with jagged edges on one side, hastily torn out to scribble on. Bright purple crayon markings and hand-drawn flowers met my eyes. "It will be okay. Dawson smells like a gross, stinky boy. I'm still your best, best friend." That was all the note said except for the traditional signature of the big heart with the name "Jess" inside and a P.S. at the end saying "I love your new plastic barrette."

I was snapped back into reality when my senses were jolted by a loose rock on the pavement, subduing my daydreams at once. I tripped and almost lost myself completely, feeling about as graceful as a deer on ice, but thankfully only the worn backpack suffered in the end. *Stupid, fat rock*, I thought, kicking it in disgust. I wish now I had used that on Dawson instead of my fist, imagining clubbing him with its brute strength. *That* would have surely shown him. But honestly, how was I to know what would hurt a boy? The monster's stone fists hurt me plenty, but he was a lot bigger and indefinitely stronger than me. I used to be so brave, or at least I like to imagine that I was, in a world too long ago to remember, one covered over and darkened in time. But somewhere deep inside me still, I just knew there was a crouching hero; I could feel her expectantly waiting.

My eye hurt again and I rubbed it with careful tenderness, though the pain only intensified. It was enormous now, even more than it had been right after the fight, though at least the crimson blood had finally dried. "Oh no," I thought incredulously, and the dread of home hit me like a board to the face. How was I almost there *already*? Just one more ordinary house separated us, one I'd walked past many times, but never really noticed before.

An unfamiliar voice suddenly filled the air, snapping me out of my dread before I even knew what was happening. It was deep and melodic, sounding as though it was brimming with magical stories and tales of wonder. "Looks like you had a rough day, little girl." I was so startled, so taken aback, that my invisible frame actually fell down this time. It was distinctively a man's voice and from my experience, that was never a good thing, not even a tiny little bit.

Plucking myself up off the ground, I scanned for the source, my searching eyes finally resting on the front porch of the gingerbread house next to me, where two older people sat; looking as foreign to me as anyone I had ever seen. Their skin looked like it had been burnt, beautifully dark and toasty-colored. I walked up the sidewalk to their house, stopping just short of the front steps and looked down again at their dreamlike, silky skin, feeling my one good eye grow massive.

"Looks like you had a worse one than me, you burnt old man." I watched his face contort and contemplated if I had made him mad. I seriously hoped so. All men were undoubtedly evil as far as I was concerned. But as I intensely looked at him, deep lines of sweetness began to form around his mouth as a broad smile emerged. I, obviously, was unendingly disappointed.

"You've never seen anyone that looks like me before, have you?" he asked, already knowing the answer.

"No," I said, exasperated at the peppering questions. I walked onto the first step, filled with wonder, still staring, sure my eyes were going to pop out of my head. This time he looked at the old woman, amused but trying to hide it, and they smiled at each other intently.

"What happened to you?" I asked incredulously. "You look like a burnt biscuit!" His head was covered with a big, black rounded hat and I wondered if he had burnt it, too.

The welcoming, dusky smile appeared again and it calmed me, washing over me gently, like the setting sun touching the horizon's edge at the end of a long, trying day. "Would you like to hear the story?" he questioned, inflaming my young heart with sudden expectation. I doubted whether or not to trust him, being a man *and* a stranger, but I knew his smile was so much warmer than what awaited next door. I hopped up another step spiritedly, my curiosity now unbearable.

"Well," I conceded, as I walked up the remaining steps and onto the wide berth of the porch itself, "I'm sure it would help *you* to talk about it."

"Yes," he relented helpfully, agreeing to my game, "I'm sure it will."

My head bobbed wildly in satisfaction. I wanted to know the story of skin so incredibly beautiful and where I could get some. "I'm an Indian," he explained plainly.

"An engine!?" I gasped, not understanding his thick southern accent.

Johnny laughed deeply, freely, its boisterous nature overtaking the entire porch and feeling like springtime. These people always seemed to be laughing even though they had wrinkles. I didn't understand it; mama always said that wrinkles made you miserable. I guess they didn't know. Maybe I should tell them?

"No," the old man laughed, struggling to regain his composure. "Here." He pointed to a wooden rocking chair that was just my size. The white color stood in stark contrast against the bright cherry-blossom pink house. I gladly took a seat in the special chair between the old man and the old woman, the engines with the burnt skin, feeling special. For once, I didn't want to be invisible anymore. I was happy to be noticed.

"An In-d-ian. It means that my ancestors, the people that I come from, had skin just like this and they passed it on to me. Just like you have white skin, some people have black skin, some people have Indian skin, and some people have a mix between them all."

The rocking chairs squeaked loudly in the sudden quiet. For once, I was strangely speechless. I saw the old man studying the porch floor with great interest. He seemed to be thinking before his voice echoed again.

"You know your friend that you walk with a lot? The one with the bright red hair?"

"Yes," I answered vaguely, rocking idly. I couldn't understand why he was asking about this when I was trying to talk about burnt, beautiful skin here. "That is Jessica. She is my most very best friend," I answered, feeling my small chest puff up a little. I still couldn't believe it; I actually had a friend.

"Jessica... what a pretty name. Well, Jessica has red hair and you have brown hair. It is what you were born with that was passed down from your parents. It's the same with your skin, and with mine."

I suddenly thought the old man was a very good explainer. "I sure do love Jessica's hair!" I told him, my little legs rocking in repeated rhythm. "She looks like The Little Mermaid."

"But you also like your brown hair right?"

I smiled fervently, pleased he had asked. "Oh yes! My hair looks like

Belle's!"

His eyebrows furrowed at the name. "Belle's?" I looked at him like he had six chins, like he was undoubtedly worse than the bumper sticker mom.

"*Belle* off of Beauty and the Beast?" The old woman next to me whispered, "The Disney movie."

I sighed in relief that someone remembered her and thought it strange that she said so little. When she did speak, though, it was always very important. Like with Belle.

The old woman smelled like specks of gingerbread and gummy bears, like scraps of cinnamon rolls and sugar cookies, like fresh-baked cupcakes covered in frosting. I breathed her in appreciatively. I was so hungry now. Her voice, like the rest of her, was quiet and gentle. She had the kind of voice that would be lost altogether if the wind blew too loudly. I wondered how these two ever ended up together. Then the old man silently reached for her hand and she gave it to him, freely, with nothing but a soft smile. I knew there must be something there that I was too young to understand.

"Oh," the old man's face finally registered delayed recognition. "That is my granddaughter Emily's favorite movie. She has hair like Belle's too."

"She's like Belle? Oh, she must be so lovely!" I exclaimed in unbridled delight.

"Yes, she is," he agreed. "That is even her rocking chair you are sitting in." He pointed towards me with a grin.

"It's very comfy," I said, rocking with extra enthusiasm. "This is the first time I've ever sat in one."

"I'm glad you are enjoying it." He looked at me slyly, then paused. "And how about that black eye? Is that a first too?"

I studied him carefully for a moment. His ears, I thought, were exceptionally big, but I liked them very much. They were endearing, the kind of ears you wanted to whisper secrets into. I officially decided that old man Engine was the first man I ever trusted.

"Will you be here tomorrow?" I questioned hopefully.

"We're retired," he said, his soft, dark eyes meeting mine.

"What does it mean to be tired twice?" I asked, clueless in every way.

Again came the smile surrounded by the lines of time. "It means that we are here all day, every day."

"Good." I sighed heavily, visibly relieved.

I didn't have enough time to tell them the whole story right now. I still had to get home and cover the darkening bruise.

"I'll tell you all about it later. But yes it was!" I began to skip down the steps, the scent of frosted cupcakes still lingering in my nose.

"It was what?" the old man wondered aloud, his perfect skin glowing in the sunlight.

"The first time!" I yelled over my shoulder as I reached the street's sidewalk once again. "For black eyes and rocking chairs!"

Laughing

The next morning, I woke up on the polished hardwood floors of my living room with dark red blood gushing from my half-open mouth. My limp, heavily weighted arms felt like bricks and I struggled to move, trembling and groaning with each effort. I heard a puny, sluggish moan and it took a long moment for me to realize with surprise that it was my own. It sounded snarled, distant, harrowing, like an animal, not like a little girl in a new pair of white shorts and a secondhand Beauty and the Beast t-shirt.

From my eye level on the floor, I saw shoes enter the room: bright blue Coach high heels that had never been worn before. Their click clack echoed strongly across the hardwood floors, intensifying my splintered headache, and I closed my eyes with supreme dread. I knew my mother was drawing near: dusting rag in hand, sparkling smile on her pretty face. I watched her dance around the room, prancing gleefully in her heels, the lyrics of "Ain't No Mountain High Enough" playing quietly in the background.

Dusting the not-at-all-dusty TV, she began to hum along, her fitted cashmere blouse clinging to her curves tightly as she moved. When satisfied, she moved on to the coffee table, bending down with her perched polishing rag before noticing the cowering child whimpering in hushed tones beside it.

"Oh, Julia!" she exclaimed, frustratingly exasperated, her blue-gray eyes piercing me through, "Are you *still* there?" I saw the rage building inside her as she heaved her cleaning rag at me. "Get up, trash," she growled, muttering poisonous curse words under her breath, her roguish eyes staring at me in contempt. "You're already late for school. I don't want them calling me again. I've been bothered enough because of you." I felt her flawlessly manicured nails dig into my skin and draw fresh, rose-colored blood. I wailed and screamed out terribly, exhaling in desperate gulps.

"Shut up!" Her enraged screams exploded like a bomb in the night, shaking the air all around us. A hard slap knocked me to the ground again, and my fragile body grunted and seized. I covered my mouth with my tiny hands in fear, begging my throat not to make the noise it couldn't help but to make, a high-pitched, barking yelp. Her nails dug in deeper and I howled in gushing pain, watching as the dark blood trickled to the ground like a slow-moving waterfall.

"Stop it!" she shrieked again, but it was too late. I could hear his pounding footsteps nailing a path down the hall and I wet myself in crippling fear. At that moment, I finally lost all control and began to bellow even louder, the roaring outcry of a lion, because I knew what was coming, knew what he had done to me just last night in this exact same spot. I crumpled instinctively into a ball, the edges of my small body folding into each other, and covered my bloodied, drooping eye. "Don't hurt me," I cried, raising my hands to my face, "Please, don't."

The monster reached down and struck me like lightning, singeing my hope, grabbing me sideways with one hand by the hair, and ripped me angrily off the floor. He held me midair while my shirt choked me, shaking me like a violent, sudden earthquake. "You are so stupid! Shut up! Don't you ever wake me up again!" A clump of my hair began to tear off harshly, and I pulled away, our bodies thrashing and crashing against one another like cymbals. "You *idiot!*" he barked, the shadows in his dead eyes suddenly visible. The hair from my scalp finally ripped off completely and I began to grab my head, the mind-numbing pain raking me over the coals. I could feel the thick, hot blood on my hands, and my fingers stuck together, their texture syrupy and viscid to the touch.

Everything in my body gave way as the monster continued with newfound energy, swinging and kicking and punching repeatedly, his iron knuckles a tornado around me, stormy and unstoppable, dark with fury. I gave up, my weary heart surrendering, my tired soul finally relinquishing, greeting my ending with resignation. My unfocused eyes glazed over, and I didn't consciously see the monster anymore.

Instead, I pictured the few things that I loved completely: Wammie, with her realistic, wrinkled baby doll features; Jessica, a bright, freckle-spotted ray of light to my world, and the Engines, smelling of lovely, fresh cupcakes and teaching me of unbridled laughter. One last, firm kick brought a rush of gushing blood from my mouth, the dam suddenly opening, and I choked trying to push it all out. My eyes began to close for what I knew would be the last time, black circles of hope signaling the end. "Meet me in Heaven," I breathed out, to Wammie, to Jessica, to the Engines, the milky twilight calmly meeting my soul.

Just then, the monster's rage ceased, its cycle finally complete. "Get up, you piece of trash!" he said aimlessly as he walked into the kitchen, grabbing a dirty hat off the dining room table and flinging it towards me. "Cover the bruise, idiot!" he savagely yelled, grabbing a beer from the fridge and chugging it down in one hurried, sloppy gulp. "I don't want you here! Go to school!" As he continued to scream obscenities, I silently laid on the floor, half-dead, praying that he'd forget about me, praying that the milky twilight would surround the invisible girl again, like a blanket of welcome comfort, and finally take her home.

Her tranquil, lavender blue eyes grew enormous when she saw me stumble out of my house, the terror still crashing and swirling around in my mind. "Julia!" Jessica exclaimed, shocked and utterly horrified. I gave her a sharp look that made her stop immediately.

"Please don't," I pleaded, knowing there was no time to explain. "We have to go." I scurried as rapidly as my injured, raw legs would let me, the edges of my exposed wounds taking on air, making them feel like a gritty sandstorm. As I hurried down the empty sidewalk and away from the house of horrors, Jessica stood in place, gawking, frozen by my open welts and caked on blood. "Jessica," I seethed, embarrassed and indignant, my solemn eyes saying more than my words, "We need to move."

Finally, she understood how serious I was and ran up beside me quickly, graciously holding my tattered arm to help me stand. "Are you okay?" she asked me tentatively, though we both knew the answer was no. "Did Dawson come back, Julia? Did he come to your house after school yesterday?"

I kept walking in deafening, foreboding silence, unsure what my answer was going to be, the flashes of Heaven still seeming so close. I wasn't going to lie, but I didn't know if I could trust her either, not with something so much bigger than us both. "Jessica," I said, my tight, long face feeling worn and faint, "I don't think I am going to school today."

"But Julia! You have to. You can't let Dawson stop you from going. Besides, you'll get in trouble. They will probably even make you go to the principal's office!" I knew she was undoubtedly right, but I really didn't care at all. I just needed to get away, to find a sliver of stillness, a breath of life, a place to hide in the light fog of the early morning. I knew I couldn't trust anyone besides old man Engine to soften the fear and his wraparound porch sat disappointingly empty. "Just let me go already, Jessica. Don't worry about it. Stop following me."

"Julia, why are you being like this? I will just tell Mrs. Kellerman that Dawson needs to be put in a different class. Maybe she will do it."

I looked at her, unrelenting doubt playing across my face. "You mean the same Mrs. Kellerman who left us outside alone on the playground so that she could talk on her cell phone? I think we both saw how that one worked out. She can't help me." I threw a stone along the ground and watched it bounce into the street, skipping along a few times before coming to a full rest. "She won't help me," I revised, knowing it was the sad truth.

"Julia," Jessica stopped me mid-step and made me sit down on the sidewalk. "Just wait. We can figure this out, okay? I know we can. Just tell me what Dawson did. I'll beat him up myself today if you want me to." Her soft, creamy face was so earnest that, had the moment not been so serious, I just might have burst out laughing. She was really beginning to grow on me. I didn't know how she could deal with me at my worst moments, but somehow she knew just exactly what to do, every time.

"He didn't do anything, Jessica." I responded dejectedly, "Well, nothing after the jungle gym. I haven't even seen him since then."

Her face registered visible relief followed by marked confusion. "Then who *did this* to you?" She questioned, looking from my swollen mouth to my bloodied, destroyed eye to my thick bruised ankles and back again. "What happened, Julia?"

I looked at her with an exposed fear that I didn't know I could feel outside of my house. "Can I trust you?" I whispered in the fog, barely audible, not looking into her deep-set eyes.

She held up her pinky proudly, our magical childhood exchange. "Like a best friend." We both kissed the end of our thumbs to seal the promise.

"Okay," I said, my voice barely understandable behind its resistant shakiness. "This is what happened." I removed the monster's hat and exposed the thick, demeaning lump beneath it. It made a crunchy, crushing sound where the darkened blood was stuck to the side of it. Jessica's even, astonished eyes popped out and her mouth widened as she looked at me, breathless.

"Julia!" She looked like she wanted to touch it badly, but didn't.

"My parents," I mumbled shamefully, but she couldn't hear me. Her eyebrows scrunched up as she studied my face, trying to read my shaking lips. I knew she hadn't heard me so I started again, looking around before speaking, trying to gain the needed courage. "My daddy," I whispered a little louder, as she gazed at me in compassionate concern. She reached for my hand, her freckled, pale childlike fingers intertwining with my own. "My daddy does it while my mama watches."

I looked at her and she looked at me with her wide, trusting doe eyes, words escaping the moment, not seeming enough somehow. The only noise left was the deep, howling wind that blew through the scattered leaves on the ground. We watched a few swirl up and around and then land again not far from where they had begun, a trip on the merry go round in the realm of nature. "So it's all the time?" she whispered quietly, hesitantly speaking what we both knew to be true. I timidly nodded yes and watched as the pain smashed into her like a tidal wave. For a moment, it seemed to overtake her.

For the first time, she looked at me, really looked at me, noticing I was wearing the same dingy, bloodied shirt and the perfect white shorts from the day before, only this time they were covered in splotches of dried urine as well. I knew she had to smell me, but bless her loving heart, she never said a word. Instead, she smiled kindly and brushed back a frayed piece of my hair before replacing the hat on my head.

"Mrs. Kellerman is just going to have to wait. I think we need to play makeover." We stood up and she began to pull me anxiously down the sidewalk, in the opposite direction that we had been going, back towards her house once again. "I've been wanting to borrow your new pink barrette anyway."

We walked down the wide, abandoned hallway to the closed door of our classroom in fear, knowing at minimum we had already missed spelling and math for the day. The impromptu makeovers had been wonderful, so fairy tale incredible that for a few hours I had been whisked away to a world of glowing dresses and Chanel perfume and for a moment, I'd actually stopped thinking of what had happened to me only minutes before. Jessica tenderly cleaned my bruise with a soft, new cotton washcloth, generously wiping all the dried blood off and somehow when she did, it eased even the emotional pain I felt in that moment.

Afterward, she gave me a prettier hat to wear, one that actually fit my head unlike my dad's huge trucker hat. She let me borrow her favorite shiny pink sparkle lip gloss and I let her wear my new pink barrette in exchange. She even lent me a nicer pair of shorts for the day, these ones bubblegum pink, their edges frosted with white flowers and patterned hearts on the trim, and a pink shirt that said "princess" in delicate cursive across it. I loved it indescribably as I stared down proudly at my frame, shocked I was wearing anything this fashionable, this clean.

I saw her quietly throw away my pungent clothes in the bathroom trashcan, though she didn't know I was watching from the hallway, feeling incredibly ashamed and eternally grateful at the exact same moment. Jessica, I now knew, was *extremely* trustworthy. More than that, she was a real, true friend. I had never had one before, aside from Wammie of course, and it was the best feeling in the whole wide world.

We reached the heavy metal doorknob of the classroom and I paused, inhaling a deep, shaken breath, too fearful to move. I could imagine Mrs. Pierce, the mid-aged, overweight principal, staring down at me with her vacant, hazel eyes the second I opened the door, or worse, Mrs. Kellerman standing there thumping that dumb yardstick in her hand, her crooked eyebrows arched midair, ready to teach me a lesson while the other children laughed like little devil hyenas and her hair refused to move. I closed my baggy, sleepless eyes and reached for the doorknob like it would shatter upon my touch.

"Once upon a time, in a faraway magical forest, lived a baby fox and a baby deer..." A young, gorgeous, *insanely gorgeous*, woman I had never seen before was sitting at the head of a circle while all the children watched her attentively as she held out the picture book for their eager eyes. "*Where is Mrs. Kellerman?*" Jessica asked incredulously behind me, her voice relaying part shock but more unmasked relief. I didn't answer; I was too amazed at the wondrous woman before us. She was *nothing* like Mrs. Kellerman.

Where Mrs. Kellerman had bright blonde hair and fierce, bitter green eyes, this woman had dark, hazelnut brown hair and big, inviting eyes of the ocean, pacific blue and forever deep. Mrs. Keller-man was older, at least fifty, and always wore a pronounced, permanent scowl; this woman couldn't be older than twenty-five and had the brightest smile imaginable, as though, inconceivably, the world had never left its scars on her heart. She was undoubtedly the most beautiful woman I had ever seen. The dry erase board behind her seemed to glow, the blue cursive letters spelling out "Miss Katie Taylor" feeling like the first breath of spring. I stood by the open door, a goofy half-grin splayed across my face, staring, but so shy, until she noticed me in passing and stopped reading, a contented smile spreading across her face, as though I weren't a bother, as though I was somehow a gift.

"Hi, ladies. Come on in. We were just sitting down to read a book called *The Magical Forest*. Would you like to join us?" Despite her face, I was still waiting: for her to yell at us for interrupting, to call Principal Pierce to take us away, to suddenly grab the yardstick out of the trash where it now lay and beat me with it, but she simply kept smiling. Her teeth gleamed as white as those brand spanking new shoes I once saw at Kmart as she pointed to an empty spot on the huge, multicolored carpet, the words "Circle of Love" painted on it. I smiled back, already won over.

"Sure. Thank you."

Jessica followed closely behind me single-file, two princesses parading in a banquet hall, and we both eyed one another in sudden excitement. I didn't know why this lovely woman was here, but already I loved her with abandon. I looked into her eyes again as though it might disappear, but it was still there. As she stared at me, I saw something that stirred me from the inside out; I could almost see her thoughts, and it was as plain as day, she thought I had worth.

"Thank you for joining us, girls," she said, her tiny, diamond dimples flashing our way.

Then she looked back to the other children and continued on, turning to the next page. "The fox and the deer were the best of friends and spent lots of time together, even though they were from very different homes." Jessica and I sat, utterly entranced, hanging on every word of a woman whose attention and kindness we so desperately wanted.

I heard whispers surround me from the other kids, of how Mrs. Kellerman was fired because of what happened with Dawson and me on the jungle gym at recess yesterday. I saw Dawson sitting in the far back corner of the love rug watching me, but even he couldn't wipe the happy grin I had away. I was so very thankful to Jessica that she had made me come to school after all; I was glad I had the chance to meet this woman full of laughter and life. I was glad I got to meet Katie Taylor.

After the end of the enchanting tale of the baby fox and deer, the love circle dismissed for lunchtime. The classroom emptied at the shrill shriek of the bell, with the exception of Dawson, who I refused to look at, as the kids ran haphazardly down the hall with pure excitement, dreaming of cheeseburgers and fries, of secret trading, of playing handheld video games in competition. Dawson stumbled over to my desk silently, almost as if it were an accident, his chestnut eyes looking down at his green lace up shoes ashamedly. I sat in the abandoned classroom awkwardly, continuing to stare at him as he stood there out of place, neither of us saying one of the thousand words running through our minds. It was the first time I'd ever really been alone with a boy and I didn't know what to say— much less to him, of all boys.

Finally, his face met mine and I saw that his never-ending eyes were filled with unsuppressed tears. "I'm really sorry Julia," he said, his too-old stare tracing the ground again before meeting my gaze. "I'm so sorry that I hurt you." I watched as a single tear dripped down from his eye, onto his nose, past his thin lips, and fell right onto the hand I had propped on my desk. He then quickly walked out the door, half-running and tripping on his own feet, leaving me without another word. I sat there thinking for a moment, holding my hand to my mouth unconsciously, the wet sensation of his salty, bitter tear resting on my bottom lip like a welcome escape. Soon after, I could hear one little set of footsteps stumbling down the hall. I smiled, admitting the gesture was nice of him and that maybe I might sit with him at lunch. *Maybe.*

Then I realized that unlike most days, when I got up early to pack my own lunch secretly, I didn't have one at all today. I sat in my encasing desk, feeling my stomach rumble like distant thunder, not knowing what to do. Mrs. Taylor had been in the hall, waving, watching the kids go on their ways when she swiftly turned around, her movements as graceful as a ballerina, and noticed I was still crammed in my seat. "Well, hi there, sweet girl" she said, bending down to my level, smiling at me like I was anything but the thick grease stain on the world I felt like. I looked again at her incredible, mesmerizing eyes and I couldn't help but stare. They were the exact, perfectly clear color of the ocean.

I had seen it only once before, when I was four, and it was the one memory I had with the monster before the abuse began soon after. I'd held it like a secret for years, tucked into my memory like a hidden treasure, but I had never told anyone about it. "Hi," I finally mumbled out, still thinking of the glistening waves that covered my bare feet and the way it felt to have my toes in the hot summer sand as I ran along the empty shore, laughing with abandon.

"Are you not hungry today?" she asked inquisitively, sitting beside me in a plastic chair made for an eight-year-old. I wanted to answer her honestly, but didn't know what to say. I looked down and my thumbs became very interesting. I noticed her look at my clear backpack and then at my desk, noting the absence of any paper sack or lunchbox. In the background, her cellphone ringer tinkled with Tchaikovsky's *Swan Lake Suite,* but she didn't even seem to notice. "Well," she said kindly, her bright eyes smiling as much as her light pink mouth, "I am so glad you joined me today. I sure did want some company." I sheepishly looked up at her again as she walked back to her desk, her presence still floating over me like a cool, welcome breeze.

"See, I have this *really* big problem. I had a huge breakfast and I am just so stuffed I don't think I could take another bite, but you see, I brought a lunch that is going to ruin if I can't find anyone to eat it during the next hour and I'd just so hate for it to go to waste." She paused as though waiting for something, and I felt my eyes grow wide, but tried to scrunch them up like the sweet little Asian girl who sits beside me during class. "Really?" I asked, trying so hard not to sound excited that I found myself clenching my desk with a sumo wrestler grip.

She brought it to my desk and set it down, every part of me feeling like a firecracker, ready to burst and glow. "Yes... so, Julia, right?" I smiled until I thought my face would fall off. "Yes!" I breathed out, abundantly delighted. This beautiful woman with the eyes of the ocean knew my name. "So Julia, if you could help me out and eat this, I would be so appreciative."

Five minutes, three napkins, and two juices later I had eaten a delicious turkey and cheese sandwich, a mini bag of Lays barbecue potato chips, and a cup full of pure, delectable strawberries that were so fresh I'd felt as though I'd picked them straight from the vine. I watched Ms. Taylor watching me, and I smiled at her with genuine joy, red speckles of new strawberries dotting my small chin. Her touched, contented expression told me that she enjoyed seeing me eat the food more than she would have eating it herself.

When a tiny, little girl-sized burp abruptly slipped out on accident a minute later, we both grabbed our sides and laughed in bundles until there was no noise, but only happy streams of tears. It was the first time since that distant day at the ocean, the only other time I had seen that perfect shade of crystal clear blue, that I could ever remember laughing.

Tea Party

A fter school that day, I bustled in the front door of the steamy, grimy house to find what had always been my biggest fear come to life: the monster's dark moss green eyes staring straight back into mine, a hunter locking eyes with its prey. I was visibly shocked, shaken that he wasn't in his well-worn recliner watching TV with an upturned, half-empty beer held loosely in his hand, foam dripping onto the floor. It was how I had found him every other day when I got home.

Today, as soon as I opened the door, his huge, tall body was towering over me, looming expectantly, as he closed the door behind me with a bang. I searched hysterically for my mother, the dreaded fear building in my chest like a bubbling volcano, but didn't see her anywhere. The house was oddly quiet and unpleasantly stiff; I could hear my own rapid breaths as he stared at me for what seemed like forever, an eternal prelude to pain.

His iron hands reached down and removed the tangled backpack, my body flinching noticeably in response. The only time he'd ever been this close to me was during the beatings and the memories infused me with a hot disgust I tried to choke back and push deep down inside. I lowered my welled-up eyes and backed into a darkened corner, hoping he would forget I was there as he'd forgotten me, the invisible little girl, so many times before. The monster studied me determinately, his hollowed, stalking figure surrounding me, a sick, twisting motion playing at the edges of his upturned mouth. "Julia," he said, his raspy voice crashing into me like an avalanche, desperately thick and filled with unbridled want. "It's time for our tea party."

I pushed down on the hardwood floor and backed further into the corner, unable to move another inch. "I don't want to," I spat out in panic, frantically trying to stop what I knew was coming. His smile and his patience disappeared in one strike of lightning and his evil hands grabbed me, throwing me over his shoulder, his stomps shaking me with every tread down the hall to the bathroom. I heard the gushing water already running before we even reached it, a sound that I had learned to hate, and I tensed up like a statue.

When we entered the outdated bathroom, he began to forcefully strip me down, lurching and pulling and yanking at my clothes. "Come on, let's take a bath," he half-muttered, commencing his terrible acting role, touching the back of my silk-soft hair. I pulled away and rushed to leave, the prey staging an escape attempt, but he blocked the doorway easily. I could see on his lava red face that it was making him angry, pushing him to the point of erupting, but I didn't dare stop. I leapt again and he blocked my way a second time before slamming me into the floor with a teeth-chattering slap. "Do it!" he barked ferociously, the lava bursting and overflowing.

I hit the textured, ceramic tile hard and felt the flow of blood on the back of my head, a sensation as normal to me as breathing. I looked at the monster's large frame, the air of defeat looming thick all around me, and wanted to cry, but I knew I had to appear stronger than I felt. I didn't know how bad this would be.

He sat down on top of the closed toilet seat and watched me through his slitted, harsh stare. I stood still for a long time, refusing to undress, yet too afraid to try to leave again, a deer in the gun's scope. I listened as he poured out lies I knew he didn't mean. He never meant them. "Julia, I'm sorry I hit you. You just made me so mad," he would murmur, groping me, stroking my body in unnatural ways, backhanding me when I'd flinch uncontrollably. When I'd pull back instinctively, he'd grasp me tighter and bring me closer, trapping me in his cage. "It's okay, *shhhhhhh*," his deep, gravelly voice coaxed unconvincingly. I longed from my depths to hit him and run away, but I just stood there, lifeless, like a doll.

After a while, like always, he would grow irritated with me and the abuse would start back up, like an engine suddenly roaring to life. I would lay against the cold tile wall and refuse until he finally grew angry enough to rip my clothes off himself. "Julia," he would seethe through gritted, rotting teeth as I cringed, "There isn't time for this."

I knew from experience the way this went, that it would be quicker if I cooperated, but I refused to help him, defying him with my silent, steady courage. He gathered me like a blanket and tossed my boney shape in the bathtub, undressed himself with purpose, and plopped in with me, causing the water to flow over the edge of the tub in waves. His hands, *those dirty, entitled hands,* I had decided the very first time he had touched me like this, were what I hated the most. They were either beating me or touching me sexually. When he first did it, I was only four.

He went through his normal, predictable routine: washing my matted, tangled hair first, touching it, smelling it, twirling it into funny shapes as if we were a normal family, taking a normal bath.

I wondered if it made him feel better when he did this, if it made him feel like he wasn't a pervert as his eyes scanned hungrily over my childish body.

Then, though, like always, there was more. After he finished rinsing the shampoo out of my freshly cleaned hair, he would smell its fragrant scent and say, "See, Julia, you are not a little girl. You are a big girl. You're practically a woman... an intensely beautiful woman." Then he would eagerly soap up his big, meaty hands and make me face him and I'd wish with every ounce of strength I could muster to simply die.

I never knew how long it was between when he started his routine in the bathtub and when he drug my aching, sore body down the hall to my bedroom. It felt like days, endless days, but I knew it couldn't have been or my mother would be back; she always came back when he was done, as if her not being there meant it didn't really happen.

She knew what he did, as I saw her looking at naked photos he had taken of me, ones that I had wanted to rip apart with every ounce of my being, but I could never get close enough to do it. I saw her cry, once, sitting on the edge of her bed and dabbing at her swollen eye, but in the end, she kept them anyway, in a drawer too high for me to reach. I wondered why she stayed with him, why she let him beat me until my bloody, purple eyes wouldn't open for days at a time. I wondered why, out of all the millions of mothers in the world, ones I dreamed were kind, and sweet, and supportive, this weak, cowardly one had to be mine.

We were on the floor of my room now, the monster moving above me, grunting in rhythm, as he had so many times before. I closed my tired chocolate eyes and tried to pretend that I was somewhere else, anywhere else, and for a moment, I could convince myself it was true. I would think of Katie Taylor and the kindness of her blue eyes, or the way that Dawson's lone tear had grazed my arm like a lost leaf in the fall. When that didn't work, I'd begin to hum or sing, trying to block out what he was doing to me, but then he would groan, or put my unwilling hands on him, and I wouldn't be able to deny it anymore.

It was then that I really would start to cry, shivering and falling into near hysterics. The monster didn't like it when I cried. He'd say how it ruined it for him, then get up and stomp away. Moments later, he would bring back his thick genuine leather belt and beat me harder than usual. I didn't care. I always chose the beatings. Today, though, it was different.

My cries soared and even turned to deafening screams, but no matter what, he wouldn't stop. The monster kept moving toward me with rage and I started to bleed, a puddle of shame growing underneath me. "Stop," I whimpered, the trapped deer begging for a tiny bit of mercy, knowing it would do no good. "Please, stop," I wailed again, the pain becoming too much to bear. An agonizing eternity later, he rolled off, the puddle now a crimson river of blood.

Afterward, he placed me at a small, round table in my room and pretended to have tea. My mother had bought me a porcelain set of teacups for my birthday when I was four and he gave me a child-sized table to match it. I used to love the teacups, they were the only real present my mother had ever bought me, but soon after I learned to hate them. The night that the monster brought the new table home was the very first night he ever touched me. After that, I didn't like playing tea anymore.

He picked up my bleeding body and began to set me in the chair, still fully naked, and crouched down on the floor close to me. This was the part, out of all of it, that burned me inside like an open fire. He would pretend to be playing with me, pouring fake tea in the cups, clinking them against one another in delight, but really would be looking at my body, his sick mouth twisting in pleasure at the very sight.

It didn't matter to him that I was his daughter, that dripping blood flowed from my most private parts, that my drooping face was the color of worn ivory lace, that I felt like I was sitting with the devil himself. He thought I was much too young to understand, but I wasn't. Then he would touch me, sometimes all over, sometimes in one spot; it was always different, but always the same. Always, right after he would leave, I would lie awake at night and throw up.

He had just begun to touch my soft body, first letting his hands rest on my thin arms and lean stomach. Slowly he would let them trail along my exposed legs and dance around where I knew he was going. He would pull my hair in thick, rugged chunks, hard, and I would have to fight back brimming tears. Finally, his hands rested on my girl parts. I didn't know the real names for them, but that's what I heard mama call them once. They were both so small, like my baby dolls, and I hated that he knew it. I cringed because of what was coming next, what, I knew, always came next.

His mouth was ready, anxious, and I saw him lean forward. I started to kick and resist, but he pinned my legs down. "No," I said, squirming beneath his massive strength. I squeezed my eyes shut and tried so hard to block him out again. It was then, coming closer and growing piercingly louder every second, that I began to hear the blare of the sirens.

The monster jumped up instantly and pulled back the partially-opened curtains, their lacy, flowered pattern too innocent for this moment, this room. He looked out the uncovered front window, the dread of what he saw shaking him to his core. Three distinct police cars, their lights flashing blindingly, were encircling and surrounding our front lawn, the shrill sound of sirens bringing out an array of neighbors.

I looked over with effort to see that both of my bedroom windows were open. Through the glass, I could see the woman with the whisper voice next door on the phone, tears streaming down her face, like a flowing waterfall of sadness. I got up as fast as I could, ignoring the dripping stream of blood, and ran out wildly into the hallway, directionless and desperate. The police were banging like a hammer at the front door; in the background, the teacups were shattering in unison, as the monster threw them brutally against the wall, enraged.

I couldn't let him reach me before the police did. "Juliaaaa!" his voice boomed like sudden thunder, and I knew it meant death. I saw him running around the house, searching me out, throwing on any piece of clothing he could find, at the same time that my absentee mother's car was pulling into the drive. I knew that I had to leave, no matter what. This was it. I was gone or I was dead.

I ran frantically through the tiny kitchen and out the screened in porch door, my tiny naked body exposed for all the neighbors to see, bloodstained legs and deathly pale skin, but I didn't care as I ran over to the back deck of the house right next door, and straight into the old couple's arms.

"Oh Julia," they soothed as they rocked me tenderly and covered me with an extra soft blanket. I could feel my bruised body shaking terribly, but didn't even try to stop it. "It's okay, sweet girl," they whispered in between sobs, as all three of us held each other and cried.

Cleansing

T he air was thick with moisture and fear as I trembled and wailed innocently, imminent rain looming on the nearby horizon. Just moments earlier, I had felt his heavy steps behind me, his suffocating hands barely grazing the back of my stiff neck, my resolute legs barely able to outrun his sordid grasp. The old man who had captured my heart in just one afternoon now changed my world forever, yelling out in his full voice to the police, signaling help to come our way. "Police! He's over here!"

The relentlessly pursuant monster stopped climactically in his tracks, changing paths instantly, scuttling towards the open road instead, dodging the men in uniforms who rushed at him like linebackers, their weapons now drawn instead of concealed. "Take the girl inside! It's not safe out here!" the officer yelled in our direction. Off to the side, directly in the front yard of my house, my mother stood with wide, unnatural legs as they patted her down, checking for weapons, before slapping the hard iron cuffs on her small wrists and tightening them down. She blubbered out objections, marijuana falling out of her side pocket as she spoke. "Is this about them drug charges? I done told y'all I was framed already! Those were planted, I'm telling ya!" The officers ignored her protests and pushed her head down as they forced her into the backseat of the patrol car with the sirens still wailing and the intensely bright flashing lights blinding her, adding to her state of confusion. In the background, I heard a gunshot sound off like an accusation after the policeman yelled, "Surrender or we're going to shoot!"

A sudden rush of terror flushed over me again like a heat wave and I sat down on the stained deck and screamed audaciously, beating my fists against the hard wood and fighting newfound tears. Elsie sat down beside me and wrapped me in her sweetness, the cupcake smell, the quiet voice, and I crawled into her lap, snuggling her as I liked to snuggle Wammie, sniffling and giving in to her warmth. The petals of rain began to fall then, little balls of subdued wetness, and I felt like God was cleansing the earth. "Let's go inside, sweet girl," Johnny whispered, helping Elsie and me stand up from the hard plank we were on. "I'm going to make us all some hot chocolate." Johnny leaned over to Elsie and whispered words I couldn't hear as we entered the house. She bent down and met my eyes as Johnny rustled around in the background, gathering mugs and candy canes, marshmallows and the oversized jar of chocolate mix. "Honey, do you feel like getting cleaned up?" she asked, looking at the sticky, imposing blood that covered my legs like a disease. I looked at them in disgust, remembering where those stains started. "Yes, please," I sniffled, wanting desperately for her to erase my shame. "Okay, sweetheart, do you want a washcloth or a bath?" she asked in a gentle, unpresumptuous manner. "*No, no!*" I writhed in my chair as if I was possessed, kicking my feet and pushing away. "*Not a bath!*" I screamed in a violent, desperate outburst.

Johnny brought over the first cup of hot chocolate, with a miniature candy cane sticking out of the right side, and coaxed her gently,
"Well, how about you just get the guest wash cloths for her, Elsie."
She nodded tenderly and left the room quietly to collect them. As
the old man opened his mouth to speak to me, a loud rapping was
heard at the front door and he smiled at me gently, my hostile feelings
melting away like snow-capped mountain tops meeting the morning
sun at the sight. "I'll be right back, sweetheart."

The old Engine disappeared from view and I made a beeline to the
front room, sneaking past the old man and the woman with a weighted clipboard on the sprawling porch, and pressed my stark, ivory face
against the big picture window and peered outside. The streams of
rain partially blocked my view, but still I could see the shadows of a
monster, a man, a father who was never a father running through the
open field across the way, the police in hot pursuit right behind him.

"Julia...?" Elsie's voice floated through the air like a bird's song,
pleasant and beautiful, and I turned my head at her call. "I'm right
here," I answered, my voice sounding smaller than I felt, the feeling
of someone actually caring about where I was not going unnoticed by
me. Elsie met me at the window, glancing at my view, and sat beside
me with the warm washcloth, not trying to stop my curiosity. "Is it
okay if I wipe off that stain, sweetheart? Or would you rather do it,
hun?"

I looked at her kindhearted face and the emotions filled me
up, endless and wonderful, pouring into me like unbridled hope. I
couldn't believe it. Already, I loved her, and I knew that I needed
her. "You can," I responded strongly, placing my hand on top of her
wrinkled one and guiding it to the drops of blood, dabbing at the
rose bushes of death, the unkempt vines of thorny, raw pain, my
gaze staying glued to Elsie's. Throughout it all, tears fell steadily from
both of our eyes, as the rain continued to pour down all around,

surrounding us like a shield, and I couldn't help but wonder if maybe it was God's way of cleansing us, too.

Nightmare

"**I** 'm sorry we didn't make it out sooner," the unidentified voice said solemnly, as though they'd done something wrong. "It was a priority... we just have so many cases, you know. So many children need our help. It's hard to know which one should come first." The voices came in and out of my consciousness like waves, flowing in and then drifting back out before returning again. I could only hear bits and pieces: the old man's voice, the unknown voice, the sound of an ink pen scribbling against a clipboard.

Elsie had set me up on in an oversized chair in the living room and brought me my cup of hot chocolate, covering me with a heavy, hand-knitted afghan and kissing me gently on the cheek before leaving to talk with Johnny. Beside me, she'd left a stack of little girl's books about flowers and princesses and animals. I'd never seen so many books in all my life and I knew this is what Belle must have felt like when the Beast gave her his library. Mountains of books was no joke, indeed. I held one aimlessly, flipping through its colorful pages, and wondered why they had books for a little girl when there was no little girl who lived here. *Must be their granddaughter's stuff, I guess...*

I didn't give it another thought as I half-read, half-listened to the muffled voices at the door. "We're still set up from when we were foster parents before... Amber's old room is ready if Julia needs a place to stay. We'd love so much to have her." My ears perked up at my name and the thought of staying in this castle where I'd first tasted freedom. I set aside my things, ran to the old man, and clung ferociously to his legs. *"I won't go with anyone else!"* I yelled up at the face I didn't know. *"I'll only stay with the Engines! Do you hear me... I won't go!"*

The lady was younger than the old couple, a whole lot younger, but her eyes looked so very tired. Her hair hung in her face and I wished she'd wipe it back, but she never did. She glanced at the sheriff standing next to her, the oldest of them all, his skin leathery and caked on like cornbread, a voice I suddenly knew that I'd never heard at all, while making weird motions with her eyes to all the adults.

Everyone had stopped talking, as though I'd interrupted something, as though I hadn't been a part of the conversation all along. The snaggletoothed lady bent down to me as I held onto Johnny's leg for dear life, refusing to release my clingy grasp, unwilling to be anywhere but beside these people who quieted my soul.

"Hi Julia," she said easily, as though she did this every day, "Let's all find a quiet place to sit and talk, does that sound okay?" I looked up, way up, and Johnny nodded that I should give my consent, his large-brimmed hat barely moving at the motion. I looked at him and then the lady and nodded tepidly that I agreed. *"But I'm not letting go of this leg!"* I spoke defiantly, my overly pouty lip and stubbornly protruding chin giving me the air of a tiny, premature gangster.

Heaping piles of mashed potatoes, cornbread, fried chicken, green beans, blueberry cobbler, and cherry pie lined the long, formal dining table and I sat entranced, the creamy, sweet scents drawing me in like a smile. Elsie had been cooking all afternoon, ever since the sheriff and that lady whose name I'd already forgotten had left. "This will work for tonight, maybe even as part of temporary custody, since you're already in the system and she's obviously taken to you both. She doesn't have any immediate family in this area anyway," he'd said, nodding his head, though I didn't really know what the words meant. I silently watched the lady scribbling down notes in the background. "We'll go from there tomorrow," the sheriff finished, the thought trailing behind him as he exited, the young woman following his steps closely.

Johnny had shown me a fairytale little girl's room I didn't know existed, in the middle of the hallway on the left, a big room with antique white furniture, a sweeping canopy bed, and a big mirror over the dresser. I remembered my promise to never look in a mirror again and turned away when I saw it. "Can you take it down?" I asked him quickly, pointing, and without questioning why, he did. I looked at the top of the empty dresser and felt flooded by relief. "That's better," I whispered, though I wasn't sure anyone but my soul heard me.

The old man was busy pulling on the fluffy, oversized comforter, preparing it for its new guest, its pure, milky white color inviting me like a peaceful dream. He opened the dresser drawers, revealing stacks of stuffed animals, toys, and books... even *more books! Dr. Seuss, Mercer Mayer, The Berenstain Bears,* tons of *Little Golden, Llama Llama*

Red Pajama, and too many more to even count. I reached in and pulled out one with the title *Love You Forever* and hopped up on the bed as if it were already mine, patting the top of the comforter beside me, signaling the old man to join me.

"C'mon," I said with a grin. Johnny reached for the book, but I stopped him with my small hand. "Wait... could I read it to *you?*" He smiled a crooked smile agreeably and my spirit felt feather light as I began reading, floating gently on the breeze of spontaneity. "*A mother held her new baby and very slowly rocked him back and forth, back and forth, back and forth, and while she held him she sang: I'll love you forever, I'll like you for always, As long as I'm living...*" I looked up at his angled, sunlit eyes and giggled slightly as I changed the words to, "*My Engine you'll be.*" I fell into him like a newfound love and his old, aged body cradled me as we both succumbed to a fit of giggles, the first scents of blueberry cobbler wafting strongly through the air, the aroma heavenly, sweetly balmy, like a scented breeze of flowery perfume suddenly passing by.

He was pounding on my window, his raised, bruised hand ready to attack, the large, imposing frame of his body striking against the glass with fury. Lightning struck with force outside, illuminating the deathly black night, and in a flash of a moment, by the flickering light, I saw the outline of his handgun, cocked and primed for use. He pulled up on the window frame with gusto, and terror rolled over me like a tire meeting gravel as it began to budge, giving into his burning, threatening touch.

I staggered out of the raised bed, tearing across the carpet and plunging into my own attack on the window, ripping and pressing against the frame desperately, stumbling to block his movements and try to keep it closed. The rays of moonlight faintly crossed over me, the canopy of heavy foliage hanging low in the shadows of the night, covering me like a blanket of freshly laid snow.

For a moment, he disappeared from sight, but I could still hear his enraged, daring footsteps, set in a line, plopping in the mud outside and pacing beneath the window, when all of a sudden, without warning, his shoulder burst clear through the windowpane as the rest of his body followed suit, tumbling and scuffing against the edges of the floor. Crouching and then standing up before I could even catch my breath, he bolted at me like a hungry lion, leaping and roaring, the pit in my stomach stirring with the instinct to survive.

His bulky, dirty hands found my neck and choked me, and I shuddered when I heard his voice, the controlling, whiskey breath cutting me like icy morning air in the dead of winter. "Help," I croaked out, his fingers squeezing the strength right out of my breath. "He's here! He's here!" I squeaked out, the words dying as soon as they touched the air. "Help me!" the invisible girl cried, the crunching snap of my neck sounding foreign to my own ears, like a forgotten forest twig breaking under the feet of a hunter.

"*Julia! Julia!*" they cried together, rushing into my room and throwing on the light. I writhed and yelped, tossing as his hands took my life. Johnny began to shake me gently, willing me to wake up, trying to rouse me from my nightmare. "The monster's here!" I screamed again into the quiet, peaceful house while they desperately tried to awaken me, as I slipped in and out of my own dream horror. Johnny gathered me up into his strong, weathered arms and shook me more vigorously.

"Julia, wake up!" he screamed in fright, tense and worried. Finally, I emerged from the choking fog, passing from a deathly dream to a lively reality where the loving words of an easy, gracious woman refreshed me like the promise of spring, quieting and invigorating my frozen, frightened heart. "It's not real, sweetheart," her calming, soothing voice whispered, answering the question in my heart, re-aligning my soul with what was true, pulling me back into the light. "It's only a bad nightmare, honey. You can wake up now."

The comforting glow of the fire warmed me as I sat in Johnny's fluffy rocker in the living room, eating my second big piece of apple pie and washing it down with another huge glass of milk. We were in the midst of a game of Candy Land, just having taken the Gumdrop Pass, and as expected, I was winning, but the memory of the nightmare haunted me like a nagging regret. Subconsciously, I reached up and touched my throat, expecting to feel the thick rings of marks left by his meaty fingers, but it was as smooth as always.

The old woman was distracted, watching me rub my neck, lost in thought. "Your turn," I motioned to Elsie and she drew a double green card, moving to Grandma Nut's house, followed by Johnny who drew a single blue. Next, I drew a victorious double purple and slid right into Candy Castle, congratulated by the King Candy himself. Normally I would revel in my win, but I still felt a little down. "What are we going to do now?" I asked the Engines as they cleaned up the board game, tidying the cards and folding the board on itself until it fit in its tiny cardboard container. "What would you like to do? It can be anything you want!" I thought for a moment and then knew just what sounded fun.

"A movie!" I squealed, rushing to the TV stand and opening the drawers, smiling in delight that I was right about where they kept their stash. "I want... this one!" I held up the VHS box of the funny green cartoon creature stealing a tree and laughed. "What is he *do-*

ing?"

I giggled, covering my mouth. Johnny and Elsie looked at each other confused and then said, "You've never seen it?" I shook my head back and forth and said, "Nope!" waving the case at them. "Put it in, put it in! *Pleasssee!*" Johnny cocked his head as he took the case from me and started inserting the VHS into the player. "You know it's a holiday movie, right? It's not December yet, sweetheart."

I barely heard him as I pulled down my blanket and milk and sat squarely in front of the TV, preparing for the show. "I'm ready!" I announced expectantly, as though they were all waiting on me and could now proceed. They laughed a little and pushed play, the sight of a snowflake covered mountain peak coming into sight, the tinkling music and little singing people drawing me in as the pink Who-ville arch appeared across the screen. I bounced a little as I sat on the floor, excitedly anxious, humming a little to the song since I didn't know the words. It was purely magical and for the next twenty-five minutes, the fear in my heart melted away like snow beneath a summer sky as I gently drifted off to sleep, the people of Who-ville meeting me in my dreams.

Sometime later, I wasn't sure how long it'd been, I felt strong and steady arms scooping me up, and for a split second I worried, but then I felt the kindness behind them, the inherent gentleness, and I felt my body release into them. My closed eyes drifted in and out of slumber as Johnny gently picked my body up off the living room floor and transferred me to the soft, plush bed that made me feel like a queen. I felt his lips graze my forehead as he tucked me in, and then Elsie's as she whispered, "Goodnight, you sweet girl." They turned off the light and started to tiptoe out of the room quietly, reminding me of the Grinch trying to creep up the chimney, when my unsure voice filled the empty air.

"I'm still scared," I admitted suddenly, startling even myself. The old couple came back in, turning on the night light beside my bed to see my face by its glow, and sat beside me comfortably on the edge of the bed. I looked around the room and then at the elderly couple with eager eyes, as if they held the power to change the whole world. "What if the monster comes back?" I asked with big eyes.

Elsie snuggled against me, pushing the covers up underneath my chin and tucking them in tightly around my whole body, wrapping me in a cocoon of soft and downy comfort.

As she smoothed back my hair tenderly, her touch felt like a fresh piece of heaven, a momentary brush with an angel. "Monsters aren't real, honey," she soothed, trying to comfort me. I imagined his threatening, glassy eyes flickering at me in that moment, peering over the bright flowers of the window boxes, ready to take my life instantaneously. My heart closed in on itself like the clanging, steel doors of a cage, feeling two sizes too small to hold all the pain within it. "Oh Elsie," I whispered in hushed undertones, leaning closer to her face, sure he was out there, still listening just beyond my view, "Yes, they are."

Sunshine & Sunday Morning

"Where's the piano?" I asked as though it were a secret, Elsie's sweet face peering down at the sound of my question, her high cheekbones pronounced from my low angle. We were sitting in the full church building on a Sunday morning, a gorgeous day with more sunshine than we'd seen in weeks. I held onto her like a child gripping her mother, my head resting gently in the crook of her plump arm, her presence soothing me like a nighttime lullaby. I had been staying with Johnny and Elsie since the light-eyed police officers arrested the monster, and ever since I'd clung to their old legs that afternoon, life had become like a dream.

When I was hungry, I ate. I ate and ate and ate, actually, until my full little belly plumped out and I showed Elsie. "Look!" I said, laughing hysterically, pushing it out and parading around, silly, jokingly showing off my new accessory. I'd never had a plump little belly before. Johnny often took me on his knee, a book of adventures in his wrinkled hands, and with extravagant gestures and big expressions he'd create for me a world just like the one I'd always wanted. There were dragons and princesses and fireflies with wings. I think I loved the fireflies best of all. Oh the thought... to be free and to be able to fly.

Elsie's tiny voice brought me back from my daydreaming. "We don't have one, hun," she answered back, smiling good-naturedly. "Oh," I offered simply, mesmerized, listening to the members' voices rise and fall in synchronized harmony. It was surprisingly beautiful, like a thoughtful, unexpected gift. I poked at the side of her stomach rapidly with my finger, getting her attention again. "I'm so glad I am here, granny." Closing my eyes, I listened to the crescendo of sound.

Elsie smoothed my hair lovingly and put her arm protectively around my shoulder, patting me assuredly and swallowing hard. "So am I," she agreed emotionally, and I could've sworn there was a silent tear falling out of nowhere from her perfect angel eyes. As I looked at her, I loved her, every single little thing about her: her light silver hair, her dark, even features, her painting-like face. She was stronger than she looked and even after I told her about what the monster had done to me, she refused to let the world steal her sweetness, even one little bit of it. I wanted to be just like her, overly pink cheeks and all.

Dawson, *always around Dawson*, was sitting three rows in front of me, pulling at his collar and wearing an obviously itchy, brown wool jacket. He'd scratch at his face, then his neck, then his leg, which just plain didn't make sense since his pants weren't even wool, then he'd do some more pulling and come back to the face again. Old Lady Patterson leaned up from behind us and rasped in Elsie's ear, "Looks like Dawson plum has the chickenpox up there, acting a fool like that. What kind of parent makes their kid wear a wool suit on a blazing hot day when we're all having an outdoor picnic after the service? It's just plain neglectful. You know, his parents must be as crazy as the kid that they're raising. Bless their misguided hearts." Elsie looked straight in front of her; didn't even blink in her direction when that gossip started running off at the mouth. Mrs. Patterson stayed perched up expectantly for a while, then finally sat back with a righteous huff all of a sudden. Guess she wanted some big response or something.

Dawson Masterson, in a *suit*. I couldn't get over it. Then again, here I was, sitting in church with a brand new much-too-pink dress and spandex, speckled tights on, so maybe he was thinking the same thing about me. At least he had to crane his neck back to look my way. He did a few times. I caught him once, and he pretended his eye was spasming all of a sudden and hopped right up for the boy's room. Elsie winked at me and my spirit rolled up and hid under the pew. I knew better than to let my body follow. He did, I have to admit, look somewhat cute, all red-faced and awkward, his brown hair patchy and smudged to the side. Not that I'd ever tell anyone that, even Elsie, of course.

Immediately, I began to reprimand myself. Didn't I remember that Dawson was mean, that he had beaten me up, thrown me around like a rag doll, and given me a black eye? Well, yeah, of course... but then I'd think of the way he'd apologized before lunch that day and of his dark, dazzling eyes, and of how without him, I wouldn't have met the Engines with the beautiful skin, the ones who had saved me.

Maybe, just maybe, he wasn't *totally* bad. He returned from the bathroom, and before taking his seat again, I saw him peek at me like I was a new present. It made me blush; no, on second thought, that was probably just a result of this sea of pink I was buried in, all fluff and puffed up tulle. I looked away quickly, telling myself that most likely, he wasn't totally *good* either, trying unsuccessfully to cool my crimson face. I grabbed a gaudy paper fan from the back of the pew and waved at it at myself, my little arms attempting to do the work of three ceiling fans. I imagined what Old Lady Patterson would say about me trying to conjure up a spirit and I gestured a little more wildly, just to give her ammunition for the picnic. Bless her little misguided heart.

For now, I liked where I was with Dawson, somewhere in between like and dislike. It was a good place to be, I had decided, for a girl who got weak when she saw him. It was a safe place. *Boys are disgusting*, I told myself again, but even as the thought crossed my frantic mind, I realized that I really didn't believe it anymore. *Some boys*, I thought as I glanced at Dawson, scratching away in his seat now once again, *had hair that I desperately wanted to touch.*

After the picnic following the service, we headed home, leftovers rattling around in the backseat like loose change. When the ancient, crimson-colored Cadillac pulled into the daisy-lined driveway, I found my eyes drifting next door for the first time since that fateful day, the sight cutting me like an open blade. Looking into the window of what used to be my bedroom, I was shocked all over again to realize it: I'd made it out. I was safe. I was *alive*. Now, the entire property was rundown, almost ordinary; simply an abandoned house with a weedy, unkempt yard, sporting a "foreclosure" sign near the chipped front door. It was an empty shell, what was left of a life that seemed so long ago; it was almost as if it had never even happened at all.

I turned away, shaking my head, thankful that it no longer had to be my prison. As I scrambled out of the car, my tiny hands holding the heart-shaped cookies we'd brought home, I looked at the house I could now call my own. It was light pink, of course, with twinkling lights lining a grand, wide front porch. The one story frame was unremarkable but sturdy; the yard, however, was breathtaking, displaying endless lines of pink roses and multicolored lilies that mimicked the vivacious color of the home. It reflected exactly the way that I felt in this moment: joyous, peaceful, and enduringly bright.

Elsie wrapped my hand in hers, the pieces interlocking like a puzzle, as we walked to the front door. "Julia," she began tentatively, "Your granddaddy and I need to talk to you about something." I panicked, instantaneous fear overtaking me, afraid that they were sick of me, that they wanted to get rid of me just like my parents had, just like everyone always had. I looked up at her expectantly, waiting for the blow.

"Let's sit down," she said, pointing to our rockers that we found ourselves in so often. Johnny sat on one side of me, Elsie on the other, and I sat in Emily's little white rocking chair placed right in the middle, one that now felt as if it were my very own. "Sweetheart," Johnny said kindly, enveloping my heart with his courageous smile. "We love you so very much... and we wanted to know if we could adopt you."

Part Two

18 Years Old

2005

Symphony

The flowing strains of music from Aaron Zigman filled my ears as huge crocodile tears streamed across my dreamy face. The sound was coming from the mounted flat screen TV Jessica had in her dainty, lavender-colored bedroom, where the credits from the movie *The Notebook* were playing. We started rapidly grabbing tissues from the mostly empty box that was sitting on her unmade canopy bed.

"I want that," I gushed, still half-crying, holding the box of tissues, trying to catch my shallow breath. "What?" she asked, grabbing a tissue of her own. "That kind of love. I want it," I poured out, hope stirring inside me, my pulsing heart softly aching from longing. Jessica wiped her damp, swollen eyes and gave me a smile filled with pity. "Honestly, Julia? That kind of love doesn't exist."

I opened my mouth to correct her, but she continued on, cutting me off before I had a chance. "Yes, Julia, I *know* that it is based on a true story. You've told me about twenty times! Your Nicholas Sparks obsession runs pretty deep these days, girl." I burst into spontaneous giggles, knowing it couldn't be truer.

"Well, excuse me!" I joked, propping myself up on her bed with my elbow. "But that just proves my point—1940's or not. It really did exist, Jessica. It still does...I just know it."

"Then where are our Noahs?" She looked at me questionably, knowing she'd made her point, and waited for a response. Outside her window the far off sound of thunder could be heard if you listened closely, and I paused dramatically.

"Good point." We both laughed loudly and I hit her with a pillow, enjoying the fun. "One day, Jessica, one day. You have to remember that Allie waited *seven years* for Noah."

She looked at me with sarcastic, impatient eyes. "Oh please! He's going to need to move faster than that. In seven years, I will be married with seven kids!"

I smiled at her knowingly, her face showing she was completely serious. "You know you are so crazy, right?"

"Hey, don't blame me!" Jessica shot back playfully, "I can't help that I'm an only child. Blame my parents! I have a total complex. It's not my fault that I want a huge family!"

Her red hair was pulled back into a messy, upheaved bun with pieces sticking out in every conceivable direction. Without her make-up on, I noticed her freckles were really sticking out and it reminded me so much of when we were little girls. My cheeks hurt and I realized how much I had been laughing.

"Oh Jess," I busted out, giving in to the fun, "I've known you've had a complex for years!"

I bounded off the downy comforter and towards her open door, dodging the pillow that I knew was headed my way. I was halfway down the stairs when the massive green body pillow scarcely missed my head.

"Ice cream time!" I yelled over my shoulder, and heard her footsteps descending the staircase closely behind me.

We both had a case of the giggles and could barely make it to the kitchen without falling over. Our laughter echoed loudly throughout the hallway, a symphony of youth, as we both grabbed our sides in pain. A door jolted open and we saw her parents standing in the dimly lit hallway, frustration marking their eyes. Her father walked into the kitchen and pointed to the LED clock, which read 3:23 A.M. in bright blue numbers.

Jessica looked at me, and I at her, and despite ourselves, we both began to laugh even harder. Her parents looked at one another in shock as we ran up the stairs again, the sounds of our giggles and footsteps fading in the distance. The tub of ice cream was still sitting open on the counter downstairs, its chocolaty goodness dripping down the side.

Lincoln

I could feel my mouth hanging open like some dumb cartoon character, but I absolutely couldn't help but stare as he suddenly strolled into our classroom. Mrs. Hanratty, the Geometry teacher, looked extra perturbed at the disturbance just ten minutes before the end of class and sighed as she read the note he handed her, waving her hand and instructing him to find a seat like she couldn't care less. His dark black, side-combed hair set off his electric gunmetal gray-blue eyes as he scanned uninterestingly across the classroom. Jessica and I quickly eyed one another and scheming with intent, devised an impromptu plan.

"Move, move!" we whispered, and suddenly directly in between us was a gloriously open seat, the only one in the entire classroom. He sat down between us and we kept staring, half-holding our breath all the while. He turned towards me and the scent of pine branches filled the air like a song.

"Hi," he said brazenly, his head slightly cocked to the side confidently, his perfect teeth shining at me like small diamonds in a row. I exhaled louder than I meant to, a girlish sigh, and shot a look of disbelief at Jessica as she frowned at me, lying against the back of her seat defiantly and rolling her eyes. *I was the chosen one.*

"Hi," I said dreamily, the whole moment feeling like a nostalgic memory, as I noticed the small, pronounced scar directly above his right eyebrow and wondered how he had gotten it. Something manly I was sure, wrestling with lions or carrying bundles of lumber in the winter. He was rugged and sexy, handsome and ruthless, a man filled with mystery, I quickly determined. He extended his bare, athletic hand and as I touched it, it felt intensely intimate.

"I'm Lincoln," he said and a gelled piece of his hair fell just over his piercing metal eyes. His wide gaze was unbroken as he stared, evoking something dangerously intense inside me, and I immediately forgot how to speak. "Lincoln Greyson," he finished.

"Julia," I mumbled out like a child trying to learn her own name, staring again at his flawless face, feeling like a complete, incompetent fool.

He was very tall, I had noted, when he walked in. Taller than me, but only by a few inches. His medium, toned build reminded me of an athletic track or basketball star who had been conditioned for years into physical loveliness, his muscles infused with brute strength gained over time. I could hardly bear to look at his face, as though he might lock eyes with me and realize he was more beautiful and I would lose every chance I had. *Oh man, was he beautiful.* His eyes were still holding me like a trance, the attraction almost too much to take, when I heard his baritone voice again and it melted me down. "Nice to meet you, Julia."

"Mm," I mumbled incoherently, looking at his deep blue eyes, feeling dizzy and weak, like he was my kryptonite, the one thing that could break down my otherwise indestructible strength. The resounding bell made a shrill cry as it rang, signaling it was time to change classes, and I jumped up at the sound, looking like the flushed, enraptured teenager that I was. I looked down at the top of my desk, embarrassed, feeling my already pink cheeks grow hotter, like I had lit, burning thermite coursing through my bloodstream.

"Julia," Lincoln engaged, his voice as smooth as midnight velvet. "Would you mind showing me around?" he asked, handing me his class schedule as a reference.

I would pay to show you around, I thought point-blank, but simply replied, "Sure thing." I shot an overly excited, celebratory look at Jessica, and she rolled her eyes at me again, this time in mock jealousy. I laughed on the inside, knowing she was only kidding and was actually happy for my good fortune. She held up her hand to her ear, mimicking the shape of a telephone.

"Call me!" she mouthed silently. I shook my head agreeably and my almond-shaped eyes grew big, as if to silently say, *you had better believe that I will.*

Lincoln followed behind me as I proceeded out of the classroom, and I immediately felt the dagger of jealous eyes cutting over me from every angle, wondering why, before reminding myself again who was standing beside me. I looked up at his angled, chiseled face of stone and melted instantly. *Why me?* I wondered blissfully, willing myself not to faint.

I stopped where we were in the hallway, leaning against a metal locker just in case, and opened his folded, paper schedule. "It looks like," I said, studying it carefully, "That your next class is... *with me* ....in Senior Economics." He leaned over my shoulder casually and was now close enough to smell. His scent was like a mixture of longleaf pine and white oak wood, as if he went home every afternoon and spent his time laboring in an outdoor shop. I liked it immensely, the striking image of him carrying lumber, his roughneck muscles flexing beneath the strain, hard to erase from my curious, entranced mind.

I felt his steady, chiseled arm wrap protectively around the back of my shoulders, surrounding me like a heavy winter jacket, and took a sudden deep breath in. *Was this really happening?* I looked around me and instantly knew that it must be: there were at least twenty senior girls from my class whispering to one another in groups and huffing at me, disgruntled envy splayed across their faces. I smiled at them assuredly, snuggling farther into the crook of his arm, satisfied to not hear the words behind their small, bitter conversation, and we walked towards our next class with his arm wrapped tightly around me. A moment later, when we passed by Dawson's locker, I saw him staring at me curiously, and for a reason I didn't quite understand, at just that moment, I felt my body instinctively pull slightly away from Lincoln's.

After what felt like the longest Senior Economics class of my life, Lincoln and I walked to our next class together... *and our next ... and our next* ...until it was finally the last class of the day. It turned out that, for whatever twist of fate it might have been, we had the exact same class schedule. Okay, so maybe it had less to do with fate and more to do with the fact that we were both seniors who needed the same classes to graduate, but I liked to dream it could mean more.

By the end of the day, all of the girls in the entire high school seemed to be swooning over Lincoln, but disappointment rang loudly through the halls like a tolling tower bell as word spread that he had already chosen a girlfriend. I knew it was super quick, but it was high school after all, and things like this were bound to happen when you were eighteen... at least that was what I told myself.

I rushed home frantically, breaking every speed limit known to man and Dorchester county, and called Jessica immediately. "Come over!" I shouted, squealing into the phone and minutes later, she rushed into my house without knocking, bounding through the front door and sprinting into my room. "Ahhhh!" we yelled upon seeing each other, jumping up and down uncontrollably with teenage excitement. I heard my grandparents in the distance laughing periodically in the living room when we would have an excessive burst of squeals, but I knew they didn't mind. Over and over, they had told me so many times that seeing my great friendship with Jessica made them indescribably happy.

"So wait," Jessica said all of a sudden, flatly. "Let me make sure I have this straight." I frowned at her without trying to hide it, not understanding where she was going. This was supposed to be the part where we both squeaked in joy and threw pillows, right?

"You two are already *together? Like a couple?*"

I looked at her as if to say *duh*. Why wasn't she getting this?

"Um, yeah!" I replied sarcastically, frustrated and out of patience. Concern immediately crossed her freckled, beautiful features. "Oh... okay Julia... that was fast," she mumbled, half under her breath.

I stared at her in disbelief, my resentment growing like a grudge. Just beneath the surface, I could feel the anger begin to boil inside me. "What is your problem?" I seethed in frustration, mad that she was ruining the moment completely.

She looked down self-consciously and started aimlessly outlining the design on a pillow she was holding, an attempt to dodge the argument altogether. "It's nothing. Just forget it," she sighed passively.

"No, Jessica. I want to know," I said, my anger exploding like a flare in the night. "What's the big problem with Lincoln?" I scoffed sarcastically, meanly, "That he chose me over *you?*"

Jessica looked up from the pillow now, the first signs of fury burning in her eyes, and shock played across her always-kind face. "You cannot be serious right now!" she said, harshly throwing down the decorative pillow.

It bounced wildly off the bed and descended onto a random spot on the floor. "I'm sorry if I think it is just a *little weird* that some guy just walks in and knows you for like, two minutes, before deciding that you are his *girlfriend*. You two don't even *know* each other!"

I stared at her in blinding rage, my insides scathing hot, like a wildfire sparked by a midnight flash of lightning. "No, Jessica," I said, bounding off the bed sharply and throwing open the door with a fulfilling bang. "It's you that I don't know anymore. Now leave."

Flowers

I spent the next agonizing two weeks fighting crying jags, feeling like I had stupidly lost the only friend that I'd ever had, wondering why she didn't understand; more importantly, wondering why I couldn't control myself when she didn't. She avoided me purposefully at school the next day and when I returned back to class after our torrential downpour of a fight, she had already moved to an abandoned seat on the far side of the room, one that was awkwardly remote, a gulf away from Lincoln and me. Elsie tried after our fight to explain where Jessica might be coming from, but I quickly grew frustrated with that too, knowing she had met Johnny when she was six. How could she possibly understand? It wasn't even close to the same.

The more time I spent with Lincoln, the more I was convinced that Jessica was flat out wrong. That even Elsie was wrong. The only thing that felt right anymore was the relationship I had with Lincoln; the way his muscled hand found the small of my back, the feeling of comfort when I heard his voice on the other end of the phone, those shining eyes that still took me to a wonderland. He was the only one who really understood me anymore, of that much I was sure. Only around him did I not have to walk around on eggshells, hoping not to say the wrong thing or do the wrong or be the wrong thing. I could just be Julia.

A few nights ago, I finally found out why his family had moved to Charleston from all the way across the country. It had been on one of our first real dates, when he had taken me to Centennial Park at dusk, to watch the maritime boats set sail over the dark, choppy water, and we were sitting on a covered hanging swing on the dock when he blurted it out into the open night. "Columbine," he said, out of the blue. I had been watching the twinkling lights of the boats in the distance, had been listening to the far off sound of the horns blowing in the open night, and he caught me completely off guard. "I'm sorry, what?" I asked, facing him with wondering eyes filled with questions. He looked at his hands as if they held his whole life and began to tell his story.

"I was a freshman at Columbine when it happened. It was April, the best part of spring, and I can still remember the smell of the air that morning," he chuckled a little, an out of place coping mechanism, like laughing at a funeral. "My mom loves flowers and she had just changed out the beds for spring. All the windows in our house were open, and it smelled like so insanely good, like sweet pea and gardenia were just everywhere... it was crazy. It really was a beautiful day." I stared at him intently as he went on, trying to keep up as his thoughts turned to rambling. He paused for a moment and the profile of his dark face looked like a frozen, haunted painting.

"But you see, the thing is, I had an exam the next day and I was procrastinating as usual, so I stayed up all the night before trying to cram and at some point, I fell asleep in the middle of it all. So the next morning, I woke up really late and I'd missed the bus hours ago. Both of my parents had these crazy jobs and had gone into work early that day, getting ready for some kind of big presentations. I called them both to see if they could get off early, to come take me to school, but neither of them could. They were *so* mad at me, too." Lincoln gave a sad, empty smile, the kind that you might make yourself give in forced politeness.

"About two hours later, I was sitting in my pajamas with my third bowl of cereal watching cartoons and flipping channels on the TV when I saw it. I saw what those maniacs were doing to my school." He paused for an elongated moment, time feeling as if it were in slow motion, and I thought I heard him choke up on his own tears, but it was so dark that I couldn't be sure.

"Julia, I was so close that I could hear the sirens," he whispered incredulously, as though he could barely believe it himself. "I ran out of my house and down the street, as fast as my fourteen-year-old legs would carry me at the time, but I couldn't get close at all. There were cops swarming the place and I could see them ushering students out in groups, trying to protect them as they fled and some were bleeding, but they wouldn't let me anywhere near it. I knew it made sense, even at the time, but I couldn't stop the feeling that I was just standing by and watching the people I loved get hurt. As crazy as it sounds now, I just wanted to be there, to be a part of it, to just do anything to help. I remember sitting on the cracked sidewalk, as close as they would let me get, and I could hear their mind-numbing screams. Julia..." he whispered raggedly, his voice betraying his certain tears this time, "I could hear the gunshots."

He shook his head angrily and we sat together for a long time at an utter loss for words, the parasitic guilt still eating away at him from the inside out. Other people began to mill around us on their way back to the restaurant adjacent to the dock, but neither of us could find the will to move. I could almost smell the gardenias still blooming, both of us somehow stuck on the sidewalk of a fresh spring day in April, filled with cartoons and murder. In the still, nighttime darkness, I finally heard his voice, though it was barely audible above a boat's horn in the nearby distance. "Three of my best friends died that day... and I couldn't even catch the bus."

Music

I watched him play every perfect chord as if it were an entire song, every song as if it were a grand sonata. The old man was lost in the captivating music and I was lost too—in his commanding presence, in his seamless movement, in his unmatched talent. His fingers floated effortlessly over the worn strings of the acoustic guitar, each one crossing over the other with calming ease. I found it hard to distinguish where one part ended and another began, inspiring and stirring my soul like a miracle.

Elsie watched him with great intent, with great wonder, as did I. Then she got up from her leather armchair in the corner, walked over to the parlor grand piano, and joined in just as the song began to swell to its airy peak. They played together flawlessly, a man and a woman, for what could have been the thousandth time.

Yet as I watched them, as the music filled me like the warmth of coming home, I could see it was new to them too, though ancestral and old. I was swept away, amazed at how each part was so distinct, so solitary in and of itself, and how yet it could only capture its full potential, its full beauty, as a part of something greater. I thought of how we are all pieces of music, of how one person would cease to swell without the other, of how the part that moves us the most freely in ourselves might not exist at all.

I watched Johnny as he continued to strum, then Elsie as her fingers darted from place to place on the keys of the piano. The music swept over me like a memory of summertime, and I closed my eyes, letting it take me where it would, to a place so strikingly beautiful that everything else was silently perfect, letting the melody lead the moment. The hopeful sound filled my expectant ears and my emotions felt new again, as if I were a child, the moment peacefully pure, like rocking a newborn back to sleep. Wet streams of tears escaped my soft, emotional eyes as I let the notes take their full effect.

To Johnny and Elsie, music was a language that didn't require words. In fact, it exceeded them. For what was flowing from the withered hands of the couple before me now was in itself perfection. Words could only ruin a moment this pure. As I watched them, I realized I wanted to care about anything as much as they did about music.

A tear ran down my cheek as the last note hung softly, like a butterfly might hang on air. I decided right then that some things in life were much too beautiful not to cry about. This, I now knew, was one of them.

After Johnny and Elsie finished playing together in the living room,

Johnny left to run errands in his old black Chevy truck while Elsie and I retreated to the kitchen, hiding away from the afternoon heat flowing in the front windows. "Lincoln took a few years off," I explained to Elsie as we sat at the small, round wooden table and began drinking large mason glasses of sweet tea with crushed ice, a small remedy for the unusually humid day that loomed outside like a prowler.

Time seemed to pass at the pace so characteristic of those muggy, slow Southern summers as we spoke, like the hesitant, delayed drip of a leaky faucet. "Before coming back to high school and all. It messed him up pretty bad for a while from what I gathered. That's why he's a few years older than me, but still a senior like I am." Elsie shook her head slowly, regrettably, the thoughts in her mind overwhelming her senses.

"Something like that will undoubtedly stay with you forever. How could it not? It's not only what you had that will haunt you; it's all the things you never will have too. The experience of growing up with one another and sharing endless memories... it's hard to lose a friend for any reason, but to death, to meaningless hate, at such a young age and so suddenly..." She paused without even realizing it. "It's almost unbearable," She finally finished, shaking her head again slightly. "It's truly a wonder Lincoln is as well off as he is."

"I know," I agreed solemnly, teary-eyed, glad that her words were finally what I'd hoped to hear all this time. "But do you get it now, Granny? He really understands me because he's been through a lot, too. He needs me in such a deep way, like nobody else has ever needed me."

Her old eyes crinkled at their tired corners and she looked at me with endless love. "Yes, sweetheart, I do. But I also think Jessica needs you." She picked up her empty glass and jangled the ice cubes absentmindedly, exposing the thick ring of condensation that was already staining the table. "And just maybe," she added pointedly, taking my soft hands in hers gently, "just maybe, you need her too."

That night I called Jessica for the first time since our big fight, a long-avoided task. It was all I could do to dial the numbers and not instantly hang up, and she answered on the third ring. "Hello," she spurted out, breathlessly rushed, obviously in the middle of working on something important. "Hey," I said awkwardly, sounding painfully forced even to my own ears. "It's me." I wondered if she had another 'it's me' by now, a certainly understandable possibility, but relented in relief when I heard her reply, "Julia."

"I was just calling," I forced myself to continue, drawing it out, fighting my stubborn pride like a prize-winning bull. "To say that I'm really sorry."

I had a hard time actually saying the words, but I pictured the little girl I once knew who was missing her two front teeth, smacking her obnoxiously loud gum and standing up for me, and that somehow made it easier. "I shouldn't have said those things."

The line was intriguingly quiet for a painstaking moment and I wondered if she had hung up on me, disgusted at my inept apology. Beginning to panic, I looked down at my caller ID and saw that the time was counting and she was still on the line. The silence felt like sandpaper on my soul, rough enough to leave me bleeding and raw.

"What changed your mind?" she finally questioned just before I was ready to call the ER and I wisely replied, "Elsie."

Elsie was almost like her own granny in many ways and Jessica just adored her.

"Hmm," she said, obviously pleased, "Smart woman."

I laughed freely and things suddenly felt like they always had.

"You are such a punk," I teased, my heart feeling liberated and complete once again.

On The Run

"**O**h Lincoln," I sighed deeply, sitting on the checkered blanket as he pulled me tightly into his chest. "This is so beautiful."

The night of our six-month anniversary had come quickly and I was sitting with Lincoln underneath a sparkling, starry night sky. In my open palm, I held his gift to me, an impressive diamond ring that he took and slipped slowly onto my right hand.

"This is way too much," I said, taken aback, staring at the huge, light-catching stone. He smiled proudly as he looked at it on my finger for a moment.

"Do you like it?" he asked hopefully, excited and full of heart.

I laughed in response, feeling my spirit lighten. "I'm a woman and this is a diamond. What do you think?"

Lincoln laughed appreciatively, his normally tough exterior

turned soft. "I'm glad," he said, gazing at it on my finger again. "It looks great on you."

I'd never speak the words aloud, but I couldn't help but wonder where he had gotten the money for a gift like this, though I didn't want to press him. His family was far from well to do and I was afraid just the mention of such a question, even in passing, would make him terribly insecure. For all I knew, he might have been saving for months.

"Thank you," I said, looking at it sparkle by the dense light of the moon, unable to deny it was gorgeous. "I really do love it."

For over an hour now we had been sitting at the park, watching the bright orange sun fade into nothingness as the dark night sky approached and eventually covered the light. The rare blue moon was out in its full glory and the stars were bountiful, entrancing in their sheer abundance and twinkling uncountability. There was a slight, cutting chill in the air and I shivered unwillingly, a conditioned reflex.

Lincoln looked in my direction, noticing me shivering while wrapping his own warm jacket tighter around his muscly arms, "Maybe we should head to dinner. It's starting to get chilly."

"Sure," I said passively, feeling remarkably put off that he hadn't offered me his jacket, incredulous he could be that clueless, hot with anger that he would be that selfish. "That sounds fine."

We collected the picnic blanket we'd been sitting on and the basket of fruit Lincoln had brought along and headed for his prized forest green Jeep. I waited impatiently on the passenger side for him to open my door, freezing to death, but he jumped into the driver's seat, roaring the engine to life, the rock radio station blasting into the air like a gun as he revved the accelerator, yelling at me, "Hurry up, Julia!" I rolled my eyes and hopped in the other side, thumping loudly against the back of it as I plopped in dramatically. He began driving towards Logan's Roadhouse, his favorite, not bothering to ask me what sounded good. We raced down the road, breaking the speed limit, inviting the stream of icy, howling wind inside the interior. Earlier he had removed the top and the doors of his jeep, when it was still balmy and warm outside, and I was suffering miserably, wishing he had left them on.

"Lincoln," I yelled loudly over the pounding, pulsating sound of the subwoofer. "Can we please stop?" I pleaded, "Let's put the doors on. It's too cold." He glanced at me apathetically, unconcerned, and fiddled with the radio, the jeep picking up speed at a clip, the piercing air slicing right through me. "Oh, don't be such a baby. It's not even that bad. Besides, you should've thought to bring a jacket."

The words hit my ears like a defendant hearing his sentence at trial, understood but not quite comprehended. *Did he really just say that?* Never before had he acted this way and for the life of me, I couldn't understand what was going on with him. *Why now? Why on our anniversary of all days?*

Twenty minutes later, we reached Logan's and came to an abrupt stop, my perfectly crafted hairstyle now a complete knotted, tangled mess. He turned off the engine as if nothing had happened and I sat silently, stewing, looking straight ahead into the bright lights of traffic, seething at his cruelty, my innards on fire. I was relieved we had reached the restaurant so that the painful wind would stop biting at me like a piranha, so I could warm up a little inside, but I was so rushed with fury that I didn't want to go anywhere with him.

"Ready?" he said effortlessly, gathering his things, oblivious to my anger.

"Mmhmm," I barely mumbled, stumbling out of the car in my too high high heels, the arches of my feet begging for relief they wouldn't get.

Dinner was achingly quiet, filled with broken promises and disappointment, just like the twangy country music playing over the loudspeakers. Lincoln kept eating peanuts and throwing the shells onto the floor beneath our feet. Once he threw one right at me, and though I assumed he was probably joking, I just about lost it right there. *So classy*, I thought. *Great anniversary choice.*

The food was mouthwatering, the rolls unbelievably fresh, but I could barely eat, only able to focus on the striking, sudden ways that Lincoln had changed. Usually he was considerate and loving, even tender, but now he was just being so vicious and barbaric. It was as if someone had flipped an evil switch and he was a completely different man than the one who'd been by my side for over half a year. Sure, like any couple, we'd had our disagreements and our fights, but until this very moment, he'd never once been just completely uncaring.

After the world's longest dinner, we went back to the Jeep and still, unimaginably, Lincoln refused once again to put the doors back on. Out of sheer unbridled frustration, I reached for them myself, my black satin dress and pink stilettos seeming comically out of place.

"It's too cold," I reminded him, as calmly as I could muster. Beginning with the doors first and finishing with the roof, I attached them all quickly and got inside, already feeling the temperature rise substantially, my extremities coming to life once again.

"See? Isn't that better?" I prompted gently, trying to smooth out and salvage the disastrous night.

At my words, a frenzied, maddening storm brewed in Lincoln's eyes, one that I had seen only once before, long ago, swirling and burning the air like crimson ash, straight from the monster. The air was thunderstruck with silence, foreshadowing, death-filled stillness, like the last breath of normalcy before a tornado hits with force, changing the world of everyone in its destructive path.

"I said that you were *fine!*" he screamed with venom, punching fiercely straight into the air, busting open the vinyl roof on impact, the sound startling me like a siren in the night.

I backed away from him, against the clear door on my side and started to cry, shaking despite myself, feeling like a trapped and threatened animal. "Lincoln, what are you *doing?*" I asked with hostility, fearful of the man whom I no longer knew.

"Julia," he burst out, staring me down with dangerous, burning eyes. "*Stop crying!* You just had to ruin a perfectly good night, didn't you? You're so selfish!"

I felt my face scrunch up as my soft eyes cried oceans of salty, bitter tears and he hit the steering wheel in responsive infuriation. "Whatever!" he exploded, reacting like the jerk that I now knew he was.

"Just take me home," I demanded shakily, my limbs weak and exhausted, the backs of my hands wiping at my face like a windshield expelling rain.

"No!" he controlled, starting the car and squealing the tires as he abruptly backed out of the parking lot, his sweaty hands gripping the steering wheel and literally shaking with contempt.

"We are *going* to finish tonight." I pushed against the door with my body, its weight crinkling the thin vinyl door, though I knew I was already as far away as I possibly could be. Secretly, I reached for my purse hidden beneath the seat and carefully took out my cell phone. As I began to text Jessica for help, the screen lit up against the dark black night like a distress flare in the forest. "No!" he yelled, struggling against me while still driving, whipping haphazardly around corners and other cars. At least three people honked as we sped through the flashing lights of nighttime, narrowly avoiding crash after crash, trading one form of danger for another. Finally, the strength of his hands crushed mine and the phone fell with a dull thud into the floorboard of the Jeep.

"I need to call!" I screamed out angrily as his fast driving slung me around the jeep like a rag doll. "I just need to call," I whimpered, hating my mind for giving into my tears. The phone sloshed across the floorboard when he veered to the far left and he swung down like an eagle and grasped it in one motion, flinging it out his window, the sound of it smashing on the pavement jolting my mind into pure fear.

I was truly, unbearably, *alone.*

"You aren't calling anyone!" He struck me like a bolt of lightning, terrifying me, pushing me back flat against my seat, his tightened muscles unstoppable. *"Now sit back and shut up!"*

I laid flat against my seat, my teeth chattering from the gusty, punishing wind blowing in the hole from the roof. The fear of where he was taking me overcame me, his next steps unbearable to consider, painful questions of how I was ever going to get away from him plaguing me. It was as if I was eight years old again, trapped by my fear of the monster and his vacant, filthy eyes, and I felt something inside my bones start to curl up and fight back.

At last, he steered into a parking lot, the fluorescent lights of a skeevy motel flashing in front of me, the large 'M' letter burned out years ago, no one ever caring enough to replace it. "It's already paid for," Lincoln grimaced gruffly, "and we are *going* to use it."

I felt paralyzed by terror, grasping for any way to escape, unable to move a muscle, as though I'd swallowed an anchor and was destined to sink to the bottom with the scum, no matter how hard I tried to escape. I couldn't believe this was happening, not to me, not *again.*

"Lincoln," I tried to reason with him, willing my voice to regain composure. *"Why* would you bring me here? How could you think anything was going to happen?" We'd never done any more than kiss, and aside from what the monster had done to me, I'd never been with anyone sexually, much less Lincoln. His twisted smile reminded me of one I had seen ten years ago, on a night not very different from this one, when a monster threw me over his shoulder and took my humanity away.

"Because I've *earned it.* Six months is a long time," he snarled, my soul aching again for the safe harbor of my grandparents as if I was just a child.

I realized with sickening, soul crushing certainty that he had been working towards this all along, that everything he said had been to bring us to this moment, that the repeated warnings I'd pushed aside so easily had all been true. I needed to throw up, my stomach churning from the new truth it now held.

"I can't," I said, pushing away from him as he yanked my car door open with force. "I don't want to," I pleaded anxiously, kicking at him as he reached for me.

Looking around the parking lot to find it empty of potential witnesses, he threw me over his shoulder with satisfaction and drug me into the empty room as I actively fought him with all my might. I wailed for help, but his forceful hand was tightly wrapped around my face, making my high-pitched screams sound smaller than dry coughs.

"You'll like it," he said arrogantly, slamming the door behind him before throwing me roughly on the bed in carnal pursuit, jumping on top of me with full, rolling force, ripping at my satin dress and tearing it at the open neckline. I kicked my restrictive shoes off my sore feet in case I had a chance to run, a tiny split second of hope for freedom from his grasp.

"See," he said, watching me prepare, misreading my actions, "you obviously *do* want it." I pushed away from him with renewed vigor and slapped him as hard as my fragile hands could take, the sound startling me. Unfazed, he began to push my new dress up rapidly and his disgusting, entitled hands groped my body.

No, I thought, my mind now on fire. *Please no, not again.* I knew with every ounce of my being that I had to take action and I had to take it now. I wasn't eight years old anymore and I wasn't going to let a monster hurt me ever again.

"Come closer," I coaxed and his flawless, defiantly handsome face drew closer to mine, churning in me a feeling like swallowing cyanide. Now, it was incontestably the ugliest thing I had ever seen.

Positioning my hand for just the right moment, I waited with ready anticipation. He was finally close enough and in that millisecond of opportunity, I slashed across his face as hard as I could with the huge diamond he had given me that night, fracturing and splintering his perfect, unmatched exterior without hesitation. He screamed in gruesome agony, cursing as the blood poured free from his face like gushing water, a dam opening to freedom. A sound like distant thunder thinly veiled the air, evoking a dim-lit, wilted memory, as I fled out the motel door then, half-naked, barefoot, and on the run for my life.

Wound

It had been three agonizing weeks since Lincoln tried to rape me, and I was still shaken up, desperate to blot out the memory of his maniacal actions. I found myself looking around empty corners, skipping school, and lying in bed, listening intently, long after I should have been asleep, the thud of my pounding heartbeat resounding in my ears, utterly terrified that he might come back. He was still in the hospital, or so I had heard through whispered rumors, from when I had ripped across his face with my piercing ring. I was thankful that I didn't remember much else from that night, except running to a pay phone a mile away and Jessica picking me up fifteen minutes later, shaking with fury as she held my limp frame under the glare of the dingy lamplight.

I knew what I had to do, though I could feel the dread intensely growing inside me, the feeling heavy and weighted like a cast iron skillet. Jessica insistently prodded to go with me, even though she was unsure if I should be doing this. "I have to," I explained to her. My weak reassurances hung like a limp kite, trying unsuccessfully to take flight. "So I can sleep again." I walked down the long, sterile corridor that led to Lincoln's hospital room and, surprising us both, asked Jessica to wait outside at the last minute.

"Are you sure?" she asked, astonished, uneasiness twisting inside her like an expert sailor's knot, remembering that crushing, sinister night. I looked past my nail-bitten hands to the linoleum floor and up once again to meet Jessica's wide, warning eyes. "He's in the hospital, Jessica. He can't hurt me anymore." She nodded uneasily and waited outside the closed door, holding her post as my lifelong safeguard. I walked in displaying more courage than I felt and Lincoln fought to open the one eye that he could. Seeing his face like this now, his temple oozing blood from its bandages, his swollen, cracked jaw, his helpless, guilty eyes, slammed into me like a truck. His striking, handsome face, one that had once been so full of undeniable perfection, now looked as if a massive earthquake had torn into it and split it jaggedly down the middle. We stared at each other for a breathless moment, unable to speak, each taking the other in.

His pale, ashamed eyes looked into mine and I didn't know how to react. I had forgiven him, because I knew God had forgiven me of so much more, but I was scared, borderline petrified, of Lincoln even now. Even as he lay there like a useless lump, too weak to do anything but breathe, I felt sorry for him, despite the blows my mind felt just from standing so close to him. *I guess women always have an instinct to care for people, even when they don't deserve it*, I thought. I cautiously walked up to Lincoln's barren bedside and he reached out for me suddenly, clutching for forgiveness.

"I love you, Julia." Lincoln whispered, his vivid, azul blue irises transporting me back to the sea. He was holding my hand more tightly than I wished he would, and somewhere inside me it churned up the feeling of a distant, foreboding thunderstorm, of trouble on the horizon. "I'm so sorry," he moaned, choking the words out weakly between whimpers.

I patted his hand lightly then, the moment feeling more reminiscent of a concerned mother soothing a skinned knee than two reuniting lovers. I looked tenderly at him with sincere eyes, eyes that I knew couldn't hide what I felt any longer. There was a gulf between us now, a grave disconnect, and though I couldn't find the cutting words to say it, all I knew was he wasn't my Johnny. I knew I could never be his Elsie.

"Lincoln," I said softly, feeling dizzy with sorrow for him, remembering Columbine. I slowly removed the polished diamond ring and placed it in his resistant, unwilling hand, "This belongs to you now," I told him, looking at the wave of stitches that lined his olive-skinned, confused face.

He squeezed my hand more tightly, openly exposed and vulnerable. "I need you, Julia. I need you," he pressed desperately, disoriented at the thought of a life without me.

"I know," I said achingly, the soothing mother once again, my sad, empty smile trying to heal a wound it was making. "But that's the problem, Lincoln. You truly need something that even I can't give you."

His crumpled, broken face stared at me with questions that couldn't find a voice, tearing me down the middle, a sharply ripped piece of canvas. At that pitiful moment, despite it all, he was breaking my guarded heart, because as I watched the needle-sharp pain crossing his handsome features, I knew for certain at that exact, held-out moment, I was breaking his.

Longing

B y the time high school graduation rolled around, Lincoln had been away for two long months, the days feeling like a welcoming retreat, and for the first time in the longest time, I could really breathe freely. Shortly after being released from Roper hospital where they tended to his massive injuries, he'd checked himself into a specialized clinic for extreme cases of Post-Traumatic Stress Disorder. I really was overjoyed for him, but in a strange, heart-tugging way, like you are for a suffering, long-ill person when they finally pass on to meet the gentle light of soft eternity.

It was bittersweet for me in every conceivable way. He had gone a little crazy, I knew, from charming to criminal in a flash, and even though I never wanted to hurt him, I still felt achingly bad about the stitches he had to get. I knew the physical scars would heal in time, but I wasn't sure that the emotional ones lying just beneath the surface ever would. Deep inside, somewhere far past the gravel bank of tragedy that lined his soul and the stream of moving fear that rushed over me when our lives met, I still believed a good person lay within Lincoln and I hoped that one day he would search for him again. Despite it all, I was sure if he did, he would find him.

"Are you ready yet, Julia?" Elsie asked impatiently from the living room, anxiously prepared for the exact moment of my grandiose entrance.

I was standing in front of the full-length, antique white wall mirror in my bedroom, looking at myself in my new cap and gown, preparing to leave for the graduation ceremony. Johnny and Elsie were sitting on the couch in the living room, cameras out, flashes up, perched up like wildlife photographers waiting on a pack of zebras, overly prepared for the moment that I would suddenly appear.

"Almost," I called out loudly, half-laughing at their rushing tones. Despite them, I took my time, not wanting to waste this moment. Straightening my tassel and staring back at my bright reflection in the mirror, it felt so unbelievable that I was here, that I had actually made it to my high school graduation day. I remembered the paralyzing worry as a child, of trying to make it through the next night of abuse, the next day without food, the next hour of their screams, the next breath as I hid in the darkness. Now, I had survived them all and I was a new person, with a new life, about to head off to college with my very best friend. It all seemed so unreal.

I was honored and surprised that I'd been accepted to every college I applied to, in the end choosing the one that had offered me the biggest scholarship, from the local College of Charleston. I knew I wasn't settling by any means; the campus was heartstoppingly beautiful and thrilling, filled with massive giant oaks whose Spanish moss hung freely between its oversized branches and ancient, historical buildings with stately columns and symmetry that spoke to an era passed by, but preserved. I was leaning towards a career in Elementary Education and their program was known for being superior, one of the very best around. The full academic ride enabled me to stay in Charleston, close to Johnny and Elsie, who I couldn't bear the thought of being away from very long, though I would be moving out to live on campus starting this fall. It absolutely was the best of both worlds and I was utterly thrilled, maybe even a little giddy.

Jessica hoped to be attending there as well, and the moment she opened her acceptance letter, we both jumped up and down in the middle of the street like crazy people, screaming with unbridled joy. We had already been approved as roommates and our coordinating dorm room attire was all set to match. Our receipts from Bed, Bath, and Beyond were over $400 each. *Whoops.*

I looked reminiscently into the mirror one last time and was satisfied, my dark chestnut hair tumbling down past my firm shoulders and my chocolate eyes popping from the green eye shadow that I had dusted on each eyelid. As I stared at my reflection, I realized how grown up I looked, and for the first time it really began to dawn on me, that just maybe I actually was.

As the valedictorian, Steven Moon, took his place on the stage, a hush fell over the audience. He was the prized pupil of our school, excelling in everything from academics to sports to socializing. *The typical Valedictorian choice,* I mused. *He was also one of the kids who had jumped off the jungle gym with Dawson years ago,* I thought out of nowhere, unable to place why that even came to mind at this moment.

He finished his speech within ten minutes, a typical graduation address filled with *"you can be anything you want to be"* and the like. I tried to stay alert and pay attention to his words, knowing he'd worked hard to prepare them, but I grew so nervous with every second that passed. It was almost my turn.

Jessica walked across the sprawling stage, one of the very first, and I thought my heart would explode from pride. It was hard to put into words what it felt like to have a friend like her for all of these years. I knew that it was something that not many people had.

Next, it was my turn and I walked across the platform, shook hands firmly with my principal, and posed for a cheesy photo after moving over my tassel. In the audience, looking like tiny specks, I saw my grandparents snapping photos and cheering excitedly. After accepting my diploma, I took my place in my seat again, warmly watching the rest of the class do the same, most of whom I had grown up with for my entire life. Near the end, there she was, little Savannah Hampton, and as she passed by, our eyes smiled at one another.

We would all be going in different directions now, leading different lives, in different locations with new friends at new universities. I knew that this same group of people, this one moment we were experiencing now, would never happen again. It was just a part of growing up, I realized, but for some reason it still felt a little sad. As I watched Dawson walk across that stage on the day of our graduation, I felt something inside my heart clench tightly, a newly awakened longing, though for the life of me, I couldn't figure out why.

Goodbye

Jessica ran over to me anxiously in the gymnasium where our class had gathered to pick up their actual diplomas. What the point in walking across a stage and collecting a fake piece of paper was, I'd never understand, but apparently it was all the rage with the administration. "Julia, did you hear?" she asked me breathlessly. I furrowed my eyebrows and looked at her, wishing I could take off this uncomfortably itchy graduation gown, but knowing my grandparents still wanted no less than 14,000 photos while I wore it and they'd never forgive me if I did.

"Hear what?" I asked, scratching beneath the left sleeve and only half-paying attention to her words. "Dawson is leaving!" she said as if it was breaking news, wide-eyed and looking at me expectantly for a reaction. I stopped fidgeting, my attention now captured like a trapped animal, and felt the emotions flood into me, remembering how only minutes before he'd stirred my heart in an unexpected way. *Leaving?* I stared at her hard, almost in anger, willing her words to not be true. "What do you mean, *leaving?*" She looked at me with soft eyes, knowing what was happening beneath my hurt exterior, not holding it against me. Her voice softened and she quieted as she spoke the words, "I just heard it from Matt Lancaster. Dawson's family is moving later this week. His dad got some new job in Columbus, Ohio."

My heart sank titanically, falling to the bottom of my soul and resting there heavily. I looked across the gym, scanning for Dawson, only to see that he was already looking at me when I found him. I blinked a little, surprised at the sight, as he half-smiled at me and began coming my way. Jessica looked from Dawson to me and then back again before excusing herself, saying, "I'm going to leave this one between you two."

I was glad, feeling this was somehow a moment that needed to be private. But *why?* Dawson had always just been a friend, and yet, I don't know... it was *Dawson* and just the thought of him set something inside me on fire. He reached my side and we stared awkwardly at one another for a moment, neither of us sure how to begin this conversation, and he glanced down at his shoes, though this time they were black and dressy and not green lace-ups like when we were kids. I played with my new bracelet, a graduation gift, before relenting first.

"So, I heard you were moving," I said, trying to pretend I wasn't as affected by the bombshell as I was. Dawson met my eyes and for just a split second, his hand ran over the hair on my shoulder, thrilling me at his touch. "Yeah, Matt has a big mouth," he said good-naturedly, before finishing, his quick touch already gone, "I'm sorry about that. We've been friends for a long time and I didn't want you to find out that way. I was going to tell you today."

I felt my delicate spirit rip at his admission; it was true. He was leaving, and I don't know why, but for some reason it felt personal, like he was leaving just me behind. "Listen," he continued, cutting off my thoughts, "I've got something I want to talk to you about, but I'd rather not do it here." He was raising his voice so I could hear him over the bustling crowd of graduates and their families. "Somewhere quieter," he spoke with a quick laugh. My heartbeat pounded at the thought of being alone with him and I leaned in so he could hear my response over the buzz of the room.

"Okay," I said, committing to seeing him despite how sorely it would undoubtedly make my heart ache, like a perfect piece of music or a poem that speaks the words of a soul when the mouth cannot. He rocked back and forth on his feet, gazing at me without a word, his decidedly long eyelashes framing his stare like a picture. In the background, there was a flurry of activity, as people streaked past, their figures like blurred shadows as they went about saying goodbye to their friends. Dawson's eyes offered the sentiment that his words could not, that something urgent and beautiful was happening between us, draping over our facade of friendship and overpowering us both.

Johnny and Elsie ran up suddenly and started hugging me, finally locating me in the overcrowded gym, breaking our trance, and I felt the slightest twinge of wishing they'd come a moment later. Dawson smiled at us all and his drawl was Southern as ever as he said, "I'll come by your house tomorrow, around noon." I nodded agreeably, my grandparents already snapping their 3,000th photo, completely clueless as to what was going on all around them as my heart fluttered like the wings of a butterfly in my chest.

Dawson showed up around 11:45 the next day, which was fine with me, considering I was anxious and had been sitting on the front porch swing since eleven, looking up and down both sides of the sidewalk repetitively. When I saw him in the distance, I immediately stuck my nose in a book and pretended I was doing anything but waiting on him to show up. "Oh, hey," I said casually when I heard him make his way up the front porch steps, taking a moment to bookmark my page and set the book down easily as he waited. "Ready when you are," I smiled up at him, acting much more nonchalant than I felt.

We walked easily, shoulder-to-shoulder, along the sidewalk and towards downtown Charleston with its brimming culture and gorgeous church steeples. Together we talked about everything while really talking about nothing, touching on the weather and graduation and college plans, avoiding the one topic that consumed our minds and weighed heavy on both of our hearts.

Every so often, our hands brushed against one another's and at just the slightest touch, I could feel some of the heat from his body transferring to mine. I breathed in reflexively, the heavenly scent of jasmine meeting me in the air as I did.

May was a beautiful time in Charleston and the flowers captivated our attention from time to time, generating spontaneous contests to see who knew the names of the most. We ran through the hanging Spanish moss that freely dangled from the huge oak trees and touched the edge of hard, wrought-iron gates along the way. Eventually ending up near the water, we stood along a long walkway with a wooden and metal fence spanning the length of the water, the other side behind us lined with palm trees, architectural lampposts, and tall, glamorous Southern plantation homes.

Dawson stopped walking and turned to face the water, the corners of his face pronounced against the mid-day sky. "It's beautiful," he spoke, referring to the subtle ripple of the water as it moved along, aided by the current. I stood beside him and watched, agreeing he was right. Playing with the ornate detail on a lamppost as we stood there, I traced the black paint aimlessly and wondered what he wanted to tell me. He paused, still staring at the enticing, reflecting water, corralling his courage to say the words for which he'd brought me here.

"How do you say goodbye to someone you've known your entire life?" he asked, filling the air, swinging the subject towards the reality we were both avoiding. The words crushed me as he spoke them and I leaned against the railing, my insides feeling torn and jumbled. I stared at the water, seeing nothing but Dawson as I did: the little boy jumping off the jungle gym, the kid in class who always knew the answer, but was too shy to raise his hand, the silent tear that fell from his eye when he apologized to me, and the extremely handsome man he'd become, though he was too humble to even really notice.

"I don't know," I mumbled, bottling up what I was thinking inside me like a hidden treasure, unwilling to give him the map to my soul just yet. "I never wanted to say goodbye to you," he said, unable to restrain his feelings anymore. "I don't know how I can," he finished, turning to me and surprising me, there was just a whisper of tears in his passion-filled eyes.

Something inside me felt overcome, and the resistant, bashful facade melted away as I surrendered to the promise in his voice. I stepped closer to him, willing myself to be vulnerable, to forget how scarred I felt, to not think about the fear sitting on top of my chest like an anchor. "Julia," Dawson said, touching my hand and interlocking our fingers, reaching over from friendship into romance, "What I brought you here to tell you was I've always..."

A huge, blaring horn cut off his words and I snapped my head in its direction at the sound, my eyes growing wild as I realized where I'd heard that sound before, the memory overtaking me and breaking me away from the moment. I pulled my hand out of his roughly, stepping back and losing my balance for a split second, almost pushing Dawson away with my free hand.

"Why would you bring me *here*?" I said angrily, seething hot and ready to fight, looking over at the white hanging swings in the distance, the ones where I'd sat with Lincoln as he'd told me about Columbine, when this place looked so different in the dead of night, a place now haunted with demons of him that were burned in my mind like a tattoo. "What's *wrong* with you?" I yelled, startling the people around us who were walking by on the sidewalk, causing them to rush and look away.

"Don't you know better than to bring me *here*!" I shot out, my tone of voice scaring even myself a little, knowing my anger was out of control and fierce, but unable to stop myself from continuing. "Julia," he stepped towards me and reached for me, unfazed by my outburst, "Come here. Tell me what's wrong... please." His calmness and rationale infuriated me further, making me feel even crazier than I already did, as if I was the only one affected by this horrible place, haunted by the memory of my every moment with Lincoln.

"What's wrong is I don't want to *be here*, Dawson! I can't be in this place anymore... or around *you* because *you* brought me *here*!" Even as the words spewed out of my mouth, I could see them entering into his veins and weakening Dawson like a poison, his arms laying limply by his sides, his head shaking in disgust at the whole situation, his resolve finally giving in. "Fine," he said emptily, reeling his heart back in and refusing to care anymore, to give me an opportunity to sink a hook into him one more time. "Whatever you think is best," he sighed, turning around from me and walking away in the other direction just as the horn on the boat sounded again.

This time I barely even noticed, too busy watching my heart walk away for good, already regretting my choices, my irrational outburst, knowing with all certainty what I'd really always known, that I loved him completely. "Dawson!" I shouted after him, and for a moment he paused, his back still to me and I prayed he'd turn around, but after a long beat, he kept on walking. I watched him as he went... *who could blame him?* ... knowing I'd lost him forever, my heart absolutely, unrelentingly aching at the truth, sobbing as I realized that the worst goodbye is the one that's never said.

Free

My hands were shaking as though I'd seen a resurrected ghost, a haunting figure now returned, as I held the white typewritten paper between my stiff fingertips. Incredulously, I placed the formal envelope on top of the open letter and read it again: South Carolina Department of Probation, Parole, and Pardon Services. Looking at it defiantly, I felt my soul shift inside me, a car abruptly changing gears, stalling and pulling and resisting the inevitable movement.

Looking back at the letter once more, I saw his forgotten name, Byron R. Rose, in stark warning letters and it choked me like a gas, sudden and imposing, invading my consciousness like a fog of a hazy dream. The edge of the sidewalk called to me like a beacon in the night, and I perched on its edge, trying to strengthen my shallow breaths, feeling lifeless and unstable, my vitals rising like the evening tide. Staring idly at the yellow double lines of the paved road in front of me, I saw nothing but his dead green eyes overpowering my four-year-old body, nothing but his monstrously large hands shaking me midair, filled with violence and death.

The express hesitation refused to pass, and I finally mustered up the courage to read the first daunting paragraph:

Re: Byron R Rose
Inmate # 287418

Dear Ms. Rose:
A parole hearing has been scheduled for this offender on July 18, 2005. As a victim or survivor in this case, you have a right to make a statement to the Board, if you chose to do so. However, you are not required to do so.

I ceased reading abruptly, already utterly disgusted at the ill-fated prospect of it all. What could they possibly expect me to say about this monster of a man, this devil of a human? Just the thought startled me like a midnight flash of lightning, waking up something inside me that was stormy, mysteriously lost in deep slumber until now. I felt as if there were not enough letters in the world to form a word strong enough for the memories of his horror, of the chasm between the two worlds of my life.

Rising from the pavement, I leaned against the picket fence, supporting myself with my arms, still feeling the unguarded emotion, the flickering anger, lodging itself in my throat and burning its way down to my soul. Determined to overcome, to not give him another second of power, I bridled my ferocious angst and collected the offended pieces of my spirit, walking bravely inside the front door of our home, vowing to never give that name another thought as long as I lived.

Elsie gave me a quick flash of a grin as I entered the reading room, sitting in her dusty pink easy chair and knitting another one of her wool hats for the local cancer center. The sunshine poured in through the window panes, painting her in a soft, flaky glow, the tiny specks of dust floating in the air like hidden breaths of the wind. I did my best to meet her all-seeing eyes with a realm of normalcy, smiling back at her as if my soul hadn't just been shaken like a force of nature, and handed her the rest of the mail as usual before proceeding to the kitchen.

Once there, I forcefully crammed the letter from the South Carolina Department of Probation straight into the disposal, as if that were somehow more rational than simply tossing it in the trash. Elsie's small lilting voice was barely audible over the intense racket I was making, turning the disposal on and off again and again, stuffing it farther down the drain and watching the pieces rip to shreds.

"Julia, sweetheart," I heard her voice echo like a familiar lullaby, "There's some mail for you, darling." At her words, I stopped instinctively and felt my stomach chug like an approaching steam engine, the alarming whistle sounding off in my mind with force. "It's nothing," I whispered authoritatively to the air, "It's just mail, or a card or a bill. That's all." The possibilities hung low like a sleeping bat, covered in pitch dark, hidden deep in my fears. I felt a dampness on my pale face before brushing it off hastily with the back of my hand. *No power*, I thought, silently begging myself to be strong. *Not to him.*

By the time I reached the reading room again, Elsie was nowhere in sight, leaving the sealed envelope dangling on the edge of the end table, half-falling off, presumably gone on one of her all-too-frequent visits to the bathroom. I shrugged, unfazed by her sudden absence. She was almost seventy, after all. I sat in her empty recliner holding the loathsome envelope, the freezing cold air cutting me straight through, a knife piercing my very soul and spirit.

I pulled Elsie's sagging, hand-knit afghan into my lap and covered myself, suddenly frozen. Hitting me in the face with intruding enormity was the handwriting that disowned me, the lines and ridges of his movements still carrying my frayed scars. I wedged myself back farther in the armchair, pondering if it was too late to forget I ever saw this, to slam it down the disposal, too. I tried to move, but the weight of my own body crashed down on me like a headstone and the moment went to waste. Unexpectedly, the shock suddenly gave way to fury and I ripped it open like a wound, my eyes rapidly tearing through the rotting words that rose up from the paper and poisoned the air with their existence.

Julia,

My sweet baby girl. How've you been all these years, little one? I'd of written before now, but time moves so quickly and it's gone before I know it and well, here I am. You'll have to forgive me, I'm just a man after all. Listen, hun, I'm coming up for my first parole real soon, so be a doll and help your help your old man out, all right? I'm sure we've both moved on from all that nonsense years ago, haven't we? It's July 18th at the county courthouse. I'll see you then. No need to visit or anything, just tell the truth when they ask, that your daddy is a good man who deserves a life free from this unjust punishment. I know you will. You owe me one. See you then, dandelion.

-Your Daddy Byron

Like a volcano erupting, I could feel the massive ninety-degree weather outside all of a sudden and flung the cover off me like it was on fire. *That con artist...* I grabbed my keys from the antique glass bowl by the door and shouted halfheartedly to Elsie. "Granny, I'm going out for a while!" I burst out the squeaky screen door, not waiting on a response, knowing she was still lost in the back bathroom, probably sound asleep on the plushly padded toilet seat by now.

It was much filthier than I expected, even for a prison filled with murderers and child rapists, the smells of urine and automotive oil wafting towards me in sudden rounds and I longed for a pair of coveralls. I learned from the Warden, a man named McFadden, that Byron Rose was part of level three, under top security, where the most violent offenders with the longer sentences were kept. I was intensely pleased with that. The man certainly deserved to be locked away in a dingy prison, left alone with only his haunting thoughts as company, deserved a lot more than what he was getting even at that.

The Lieber Correctional Institution appeared to be the highlight of this lonesome, sparsely populated town, a sad, afterthought of a place with less than 2,000 people covering its entire two-mile radius. *Good grief*, I judged markedly in my mind, *what must it be like to live in a town where the highlight is a prison?* The heavyset, on-duty security officer led me to the teensy black stool in front of the empty plastic shield and I steadied myself like a warrior, taking my place for the battle of my life.

"Open on 28!" the officer barked commandingly. Then, after a pause, "Byron Rose, you've got a visitor!" His deep, thunderous voice rolled out from behind a corner I couldn't see and shook my world. "I do, boss?" he asked plainly, almost in jest. "You do," he replied simply, another typical duty in his surely-long day, as he fiddled with his walkie talkie and took a bite of his meaty sandwich, loosening his belt with his free hand and exhaling at the relief of the motion.

Byron's commanding, tall frame walked into sightline and I felt my body shudder slightly at his presence, though I vowed to never let him know it, even if it killed me. My crippling gaze rested on the edges of the safety glass, only catching his side movements and shadows, refusing to give him the trace of dignity making eye contact would bring, even once.

"It... it can't be..." he stuttered, arguing with himself as to whether or not I was real when he saw me, and for a moment I shook my head, wondering how this inept man had controlled my entire life for so long. "...Julia? B...baby girl?" he finally spit out, as if expelling the words might choke him on the spot.

I bit the inside of my cheeks hard, not even feeling its certain pinch, and told myself to not lose my temper, the same speech I'd given myself on the forty-five-minute drive down through Dorchester County, one that had felt eternally long. I shifted my focused gaze to my calmly folded hands and willed myself to keep it there.

"I haven't thought of you until this moment," I breathed evenly, the words feeling rustically simplistic as I spoke them. In truth, it was more like until I opened those letters, but the words flowed out as they were and I let them be. "And when I leave here I will think of you no more. Your actions have haunted me long enough, Byron and it's done." I paused dramatically, astounded at my own courage as I continued. "I won't be coming to that parole hearing." For the slightest moment, I was tempted to look at his well-worn face, to see if I had inflicted just a tiny bit of pain or regret on him, if he even understood the gravity of what I was saying, but for the first time in my life, he had no power over me, and that was satisfaction enough. I continued to stare at my hands.

He sputtered out an automated response, fearing his inevitable demise, trying hard to convince me with his honeycomb voice, the only piece of him that was part of my senses at the moment. "But, but Julia, don't you forgive me? Won't you help me out, now?" I gritted my teeth and delivered the words with as much graceful poise as I could.

"I'm working on forgiving you, Byron. It's a process, it may always be. I've accepted what you've done and I don't let it control my life anymore, but forgiveness and acceptance are not the same thing. I'm still asking God to change my heart enough so that one day I can ask Him to change your heart too. I've got to do some growing myself. For today, that's the best that I can do." I saw his dirt-covered, blackened hands fidgeting, moving over one another with speed, his washed out ebony fingers wringing in worry at the swinging gauntlet he was facing.

"*Well*," his syrupy voice suddenly took on its old motor-like rumble, "You certainly are a selfish little cow, now aren't you, even all these years later? I's a hoping you changed, little girl. You're ungrateful, you know it, after your mama and me gave you breath of life. Should be kissing our feet for that. *But I'm your daddy whether you like it or not and you'd best learn to respect me, you little twitch!*" I heard him spit venom at the glass barrier and a big, protruding wad of nasty phlegm trailed down its front, its slightly yellow tinge foamy and seething down, reminding me of his endless old cans of beer.

For the first time in that prison, and the last time in my life, I met those dead green eyes without wavering, hoping to lock the memory in his mind for the rest of his regretful, lonely nights in his cell, a haunting phantom of his own. "Let's be clear about one thing. You and mama gave me breath, but Elsie and Johnny gave me life. *He* is my daddy, not you. All you ever were to me was a monster."

I gathered my loyalty and carried it out of that prison, beaming from ear to ear, not even hearing his outbursts of anger slamming and thrashing like concrete against the guards. As I walked outside those suffocating walls, the small town sky seemed to open up and invite me into its iridescent blue haze and suddenly, just like that, I was free.

Part Three

23 Years Old

2010

The Heart of a Child

The steady summer months after college graduation flew by like a childhood, extra busy and filled with goodbyes and preparations, and before I knew it, the time arrived for the pivotal day of my budding career as a third grade teacher at an overcrowded public charter school. I wrote my name on the board, the striking blue dry erase cursive holding a feminine flair, Ms. Julia, and the enormity of the moment struck me, simultaneously stirring up feelings of gratitude and unworthiness in a flash.

Directly underneath it, I scrawled a get-to-know-you writing assignment for the students, the prompt reading: '*My life matters because...*' I knew it was definitely a little advanced for their age group, but I wanted to start out cultivating critical thinking skills early on. More importantly, I wanted to get them thinking about the things that really matter in life: their worth, their intrinsic value as people, as often as I could. I knew firsthand how truly important this could be, for every single one of them, not just the kids who came from broken, heart-shattering homes.

A little later, after the students' excitement had lowered to a simmer, they sat in their tiny wooden desks and pulled out their pre-sharpened pencils, the background filled with decorations I had spent countless hours on, trying to get every item and detail just perfect. I began walking around the large, bustling classroom, bending down and offering help to any student that needed it, when I noticed a girl with her tangled, truffle-brown hair half-hanging in her eyes, the name tag on her desk reading Whitney. She was scribbling angrily on her paper, dragging her crayons across it dejectedly, avoiding any actual writing, not caring that I saw. I bent down to her eye level and spoke sweetly, quietly enough that the other children wouldn't hear.

"Whitney, do you need a little help, honey? I'd be happy to show you," I smiled brightly, hoping my kindness would sway her spirit. She looked up at me flatly, as though she'd been pierced straight through, running on empty all her life and was finally choking on the expelled fumes. Her piercing, smoky eyes looked down again, resuming her meager distraction, before speaking up. "I can't answer that question, Ms. Rose...the one on the board," she explained, letting the thick words hang in the air for a beat with marked certainty. "My grandpa says I'm a waste of a life," she finished quietly, as if she knew that it was true.

The words escaped her mouth like a bitter, shameful pill, the scribbling growing harder and harder on the now torn-through remnants of paper and hitting the desk. "I heard him tell my mama last night she never should've even had me." Her fragile words expelled openly into the world, as though she couldn't hold them inside her any longer or she might explode from the pressure, as though my presence were an afterthought altogether.

I bent down by her side gently, and for the first time she stopped scribbling, her soft, downy eyes meeting mine as I did, and told her the truth without hesitation. "Bundled up in your soul, right this very second, is innocence and joy and laughter, and love and inspiration and kindness and hope. The heart of a child is the very best of humanity," I assured her, reaching out and putting my hand on top of hers kindly, covering her exploding fears. "The very best... and I'd bet that you, of all children, are even just a little bit better than most."

Whitney looked up at me expectantly and I hugged her tiny frame to me, saying the words for which she was waiting her whole life. "Grandpa was wrong, honey... *very* wrong. Everything about you makes this earth brighter and better and I promise you, your life will change this world. You matter more than you could ever dream and you're loved more than you'll ever know."

I felt her small body release its weight into me, a forbidden hiccup escaping her mouth in between inhales of breaths and salty tears, an unconventional song of sadness. "You mean I'm not a mistake?" she whispered incredulously, hiccuping again, as if the possibility had never crossed her mind until this very moment. "Somebody loves me?" I pulled back and met her tender gaze. "You're a gift, sweetheart, to me and to everyone else who knows you... and I love you, now and forever." I engaged her optimistic eyes, meaning it, the memory of being unwanted, of being unloved so close I could taste its venomous flavor once again, as if it was yesterday I was just like this little girl, and not almost two full decades ago.

I pulled back slightly and met her shuttered face, one so painfully used to keeping the light out, and delicately stroked her chin-length locks. "Right now I know it doesn't feel like it, but one day you are going to meet even more people who love you, just as you are, and your heart will feel so full of love you'll wonder if you can hold it all inside." Her lovely, curved eyes blinked hopefully, glazing over as she held up her pinky to me, the tradition apparently still alive and well.

"Pinky promise?"

I enthusiastically linked pinkies with her and kissed the end of my porcelain hand, feeling like I was eight years old and sitting on the edge of an aged sidewalk with a little girl who was saving my spirit once again. "Pinky promise, sweet girl." Whitney confidently picked up her newly worn, burgundy crayon and in an instant wrote the sentence: *My life matters because I'm loved* and I bit my lip so hard it almost bled, trying to keep the overflowing buckets of tears at bay.

Cherry Pie

I could smell the inviting aroma of Elsie's signature cooking wafting out as I walked up the front steps to our house. I paused momentarily to knock at the door and saw her figure through the window frantically hurrying around the kitchen, up to her elbows in flour. It made me smile instantly and knowing that she would never hear the door, I let myself in.

"Granny," I called out while taking off my shoes, placing them by the front mat and setting down my keys in the glass bowl, a familiar ritual. "It's Julia." She appeared at the doorway, her hair flying in more directions than I knew was even possible, and outstretched her arms, beckoning a hug.

"Jul!" she exclaimed as I ran towards her and into the comfort of her open arms, still as present now as it was in my childhood. "You're home!" she continued, hugging me fervently and patting me, the white dust of her cooking surrounding me and leaving tiny trails on my arms. "Did you have a good time on your first day of teaching?" she questioned, then corrected herself before I could even answer. "Oh, who am I kidding? You're at the same school as Jessica; I *know* you two are having a good time!" My face reflected my happiness and she knew that she was right. I loved my job as a third grade teacher, thanks to the inspiration of Katie Taylor, of course. I thought of little Whitney and her newfound hope and made a mental note to tell Elsie all about it, later, when she wasn't elbow-deep in flour and busyness.

"What are you cooking Granny?" I wondered aloud, trailing into the kitchen after the delicious scent floating in the air. Whatever it was, it smelled incredible and I made a mental note to take a huge piece to Whitney tomorrow at school.

"Cherry pie," she said proudly, pointing inside the oven as she opened it. "It's a very special night."

I feigned forgetfulness. "Well, what is it for? It must be a welcome home present for me, right?" I asked cooly, trying to suppress my guilty smile while biting the insides of my cheeks.

"Ah, ah," she said, raising her eyebrows as she opened the fridge. "*This* is your welcome home present!" she exclaimed, referring to the fresh strawberry cheesecake that was sitting inside, drizzled in Hershey's chocolate sauce.

"That's even better!" I exclaimed, grabbing a fork and siting at the kitchen table, cutting out a large piece. I was *starving*. I had given my whole lunch to Whitney today, after all.

Elsie began cleaning up the now completely trashed kitchen, putting various pots and pans into the old white dishwasher and wiping off the Formica countertops. Her work was earnest, obviously in preparation for a night she had anxiously anticipated for many precious years.

"I do remember," I said seriously, smiling joyfully, the inescapable grip of their true love holding even me. "It's your fiftieth wedding anniversary. I am so happy for the both of you."

She beamed from ear to ear, taking it all in. "So am I, Julia. He's my entire world." I sat thinking for a moment, slowly chewing every bite of amazing deliciousness that was melting in my mouth, the chocolate sauce adding undeniable perfection.

"Granny," I asked hopefully, my heart inflamed with questions I felt had no answers, "Did all your dreams come true in life... the way that you hoped they would?" She looked into the distance, wiping her doughy hands on her apron and pulling at the strings, releasing it and sitting down at the table with me. After a moment, she answered me softly.

"Yes, Julia, the ones that really mattered did. I learned over a lifetime that sometimes dreams change, they mold as you do as a person, and you have to learn to see that as a good thing instead of letting it bring you down."

I exhaled, feeling defeated, pitying myself. "It just feels like maybe sometimes dreams aren't meant to come true... like maybe they aren't even achievable in the first place. I was thinking about it a lot the other day. You know, I have all these hopes of getting married and having babies, but deep down I just can't make myself believe that there is someone out there for me anymore. I'm twenty-three. Wouldn't I have found him by now?"

"Dreams don't die with time, Julia... only our ability to believe that they will come true does. You have to hold on, sweetheart. You have to remember your dreams. One day you will look up, and he will be there. God's providence is always perfect."

I looked away brazenly. "I just want to forget," I said rashly, my eyes looking at the present but seeing the past. "I don't want to remember what he did to me."

Elsie looked at me fiercely, wanting to pick me up like the child I once was and shield me from a life that was already mine. "You're not supposed to forget, sweetheart," she said, staring me straight in the eyes. "You're supposed to learn... and if you ever want to get past it, you've got to really forgive him, sweet girl."

I nodded, knowing that what she was saying was true, but having trouble accepting the words. "I just feel like no man will ever want me... not after what he took. I feel like I have nothing to give."

She sighed loudly and I knew she was hurting for me now as much as she had the day that it first happened. "Who he was, and what he did, doesn't make you damaged goods, baby. It makes who you are even more exceptional."

I smiled warmly, taking in her words, basking in the fact that someone who knew it all still loved me so much. "Thanks, Granny," I said, before pausing for a moment, then asking her to pray with me. As I spoke the words slowly, I chose to forgive the monster forever, vowing to never let that bitter stone creep into the edge of my heart and block my ability to love again. When we finished praying, my heart felt just a little lighter. "I feel so much better now," I breathed. "Thank you."

She leaned over and hugged me tightly, the ending ritual to one of a thousand talks we had shared together. "Anytime, baby girl. I'm so proud of the woman you are. You know I love you so much."

"I love you too," I said as the timer on the pie went off, jolting us back to reality again. "Want me to grab that?" I asked helpfully.

"Actually," Elsie said, handing me the car keys and raising her eyebrows at me as if she needed a favor. "Would you mind running through the car wash for me really quick? Time has gotten away from me and it won't be long until Johnny gets home. I just want everything to be perfect."

"No problem," I replied graciously, feeling empowered, heading towards the door, before turning back around one more time. "And Granny?"

I watched as Elsie popped her head around the corner expectantly, her perfect angel eyes lit up with pure joy. "Granddaddy's going to love it," I said, and she smiled so big that I thought she might actually burst.

I walked out the front door easily, smiling, shading my eyes as the sky blinded me instantly with its bright greeting, making the Cadillac difficult to see. I found it by memory in its usual spot and drove the five minutes up the road to Speedy's Car Wash, listening to my favorite country station on the way there, though I was disappointed to only catch one song before the endless stream of commercials started. Even though Elsie had given me some cash to cover the cost, I paid for it myself, springing for the top-of-the-line deluxe car wash and deciding at the last second to vacuum it out for her. It'd take a few more minutes, but I had the time, and I knew she'd be thrilled.

Bending over into the backseat, I pulled out a few pieces of stray trash and threw them away in the provided trash cans before reaching for the nozzle of the vacuum. I scrunched up my nose at the sudden invading smell, its intense smokiness choking me and making me hold my breath, unsure of where it was coming from. Thinking it was the vacuum, I hung it up hastily and got back in the car. I hurriedly finished up, reminding myself it was worth the effort for my grandparents, wishing I'd gone to a nicer car wash with newer equipment and better smells. *Good grief*, I laughed to myself as I got behind the steering wheel once again, placing the cash granny had given me into her console for safekeeping until she used it later, *What an adventure.*

It was only as I was driving home a few minutes later, the pungent smells never leaving my nose, that I realized something had gone very wrong. I saw trails of black smoke in the distance over the peak of the trees and heard the sudden, heart-stopping wail of sirens. Turning the final corner quickly, I pulled Elsie's shining Cadillac along the street's curve behind the wailing fire trucks and saw my grandparents' house blazing in the distance, the flames crackling and spreading rapidly in the wind.

I caught sight of Johnny crying ahead, screaming and fighting off the young firemen who were holding him back so tightly as he struggled against them, writhing in grief. My eyes fixated on the dozens of bright pink roses on the pavement underneath his feet and the huge pink "Happy Anniversary" balloons that the sky had begun to carry away with its unforgiving breeze.

Everything quickly became a blur as I ran to Johnny and he fell into my arms, collapsing like a child. He was crying and screaming, fighting and crumbling at the same time. "Elsie," he cried out desperately into the open night.

The firefighters let me comfort him and began to walk away in groups, rubbing at their sweat-stained, grimy faces, blinded by the dry heat. I noticed many of them were looking at Johnny and wiping at their eyes. One looked at me briefly, and in his dark, intriguing gaze, I could see the reflection of the flames, burning up with fury the only safe place I had ever known.

I held Johnny up as he waited for an answer that would never come. "Elsie," he wailed again, his voice weary and broken under the strain. But for the first time since they were six years old, when Johnny spoke Elsie's name, she didn't answer back.

Tears

The ashes were still smoldering dimly when the early light of dawn broke across the sky. Morning had come far too soon and my eyes had yet to close, the lids now feeling heavy and weighted. I was sitting on the damp pavement next to Johnny and as I looked at him, he appeared to be a different man entirely than the one I had always known. His face seemed so old now, much older than it had only hours ago, and I grabbed his weak hand softly, knowing that there was nothing to say, wishing I could take away his pain forever.

He looked at me then, his eyes full of the same kindness they had always held, but now they somehow seemed dead, as if the life behind his eyes, his joy, his wife, no longer lived inside. I squeezed his shaking hand and fought back the big tears that rested on the brim of my eyelids that would drench me with their descent if I allowed it.

Instinctively, my eyes began to trace the ground, fearing they might convey the same emptiness that granddaddy's did if my eyes were to meet his. I worried that I might make things worse for him, yet knew in the exact same moment that there was no way that I could.

Johnny's niece walked over and stood above us, looking down.

"We need to start planning the funeral," she said flatly, without a trace of empathy, as if Elsie had meant nothing to us at all.

Johnny stared up at her with blank eyes, eyes of a man whose whole world had been lost.

"I'll take care of it, Laura," I answered her, my heart pounding so loudly it was almost musical. "I want to."

She looked at me harshly, her face holding too much anger for a moment like this. "Fine," she pouted, looking from the old man to me and then back again.

Then, Johnny spoke for the first time in the past thirteen hours. "I think she would like that very much," he whispered, clutching my hand like it was a life vest, his body language willing me to never let go.

Laura scoffed loudly and then walked away without another word, stomping her feet angrily and looking for someone who would listen to her complaint.

I thought about the day when I first met Elsie and how her voice was so quiet that I believed the wind might have blown it away. I thought about the man beside me now, who on that same day had laughter so big it was infectious enough to heal a broken little girl. Now, the old man was the one with the quiet voice; he was the one whose spirit had been broken. I looked at him again and saw he was gripping his wedding ring.

"I can't let go," he whispered, his dark eyes drenched in tears that had finally come. I pushed his fingers tighter around his hand.

"Then don't," I said.

His chin was quivering as he looked at me. "This is where we met, this sidewalk," he said, the ashes from the fire floating around us in the air like lightning bugs.

I looked at him with knowing, understanding eyes. "You and I," I tried to smile but failed. "I remember the day."

"No," he said, his lips now quivering too. "Me and Elsie."

Confusion ran through me, but there was no time to ask, for the old man laid on his side, curled up into a ball, and began to make the most heart-wrenching sound that I had ever heard. His sobs woke the neighbors and they began to pour out of their warm, safe homes. Nearby, the morning newspaperman was making his rounds and dropped the paper by our feet, barely noticing the trauma all around as he finished up his route.

I glanced at it and saw the date was August 15th, 2010. Today marked exactly fifteen years since I had met Johnny and Elsie, fifteen years since they had started to save a little girl who was lost and didn't know it.

"I should have saved her," I whispered brokenheartedly, as the tears began to fall like thick rain, covering my soul with a storm of regret. Then I lay down on that same hard-edged sidewalk and joined the pitiful old man, weeping like a willow, hoping to fill my heart in a way that tears never could.

The day of the funeral brought an uncharacteristically harsh summer morning that was slightly windy, without a cloud in the sky. The cold was nipping and biting at my cheeks, but as I strolled past the expansive tree line that led up to Elsie's gravesite I hardly noticed it at all. The flowers and the casket created a sea of pink that seemed much too bright for what was happening in this moment, yet I knew it was just what she would have wanted. I remembered when I first saw her light pink house and smiled just a little. She loved pink more than any woman I had ever met.

Johnny was kneeling by the graveside, talking to her as if she were still here, whispering words that only a man and a woman whose years together had been longer than their years apart could ever understand. I knew that he was much too fragile to be kneeling down so far and a few times I watched in worry as he began to fall to the ground, helplessly grasping at the dirt as he did.

Laura tried to help him regain his balance, but he was inconsolable, waving away all help. I knew that he would be; he'd always had his stubborn streak. The only thing that Johnny would allow himself to do was to grip the side of Elsie's coffin for balance. He was still trying to hold on to her in any way that he could. The dirt from his hands had stained the shiny pink coffin and he tried to wipe it off in vain, using the wetness from his tears as an aide.

Some people gasped loudly while others began to cry in silence. Everyone there looked on in helplessness, knowing that a grief this big had no cure. No one could heal him; there was nothing that any of us could do but to let our hearts break with his. I knew it was time. "C'mon, granddaddy," I whispered as I reached his side, holding him like a frail child. I extended my body down fully and met his eyes. "It's time."

He began to sob openly and convulsively, as he watched the casket being lowered, reaching out for arms that could no longer hold him.

"I need her," he sobbed, his eyes now as red as blood. "I need my wife."

I held his old, broken body and couldn't help but think that it wouldn't be long before I was the one who would be gripping the casket and crying out for Johnny.

"I know," I soothed, rubbing his bony back and gray hair in small, slow motions. "I need her too."

The wind was blowing loudly in the trees, its bitter gust carrying the sobs of Elsie's widower far into the distance. The guests began to trickle away in small groups, walking towards their cars in silence. Suddenly, the harsh wind calmed and for just a moment, I could almost audibly hear their beautiful hearts breaking like stained glass on the ground.

Missing

A loud, commanding knock woke me from my sleep and I walked steadily toward the front door to answer it, dragging my tired bare feet along the carpet, my wearied eyes willing me to crawl back into bed and shut them again. I had been sleeping a lot since Elsie died, maybe too much, but Johnny hadn't wanted to do much of anything since the funeral, and really, neither had I. The quiet lull of a plush bed and drifting off to a place where she still existed was too great.

"Grief," he had explained tenderly to me as we sat on the hard, formal couch in the funeral home after the service, "will hold you like a lover, so tightly that it is all you know." He kept staring straight in front of him, not moving an inch; the only noise in the deafeningly silent foyer was the steady rise and fall of his old voice.

"But then, one day," he continued quietly, almost in a whisper, "it begins to let you go, and it's then you begin to realize you can finally let go, too." He looked at me with tired eyes, ones that held the heaviness of the world inside them. "This will be what you have, Julia. You love Elsie and always will, but you are young and have a support system. Your grief, I know from experience, will hurt, but in the end, it will pass. Not completely, but time will wear the sharp pains to a dull ache eventually. That is how it should be."

I studied his hands carefully and noticed the wrinkles etched in them, as if they were the very hands of time itself, as if they'd experienced all of life since the creation. "But some grief," he spoke solemnly, aimlessly cradling his arm, "Some grief holds on so tightly that life lets you go before the grief will." His crumpled face stared at me wearily, appearing much older than it actually was. "This," he said with marked disconnect, "this will be my grief."

I sat there, feeling disquieted and empty, staring into the distance blankly with granddaddy, knowing that empty, hastily spoken words could never change what would always be true. I turned on the couch and faced him with forced resolve, "Then let's grieve together," I sighed, stifling my sobs.

I heard the repetitive rapping on the door again, pulling me back to the present, and began to grow frustrated, my patience gone and temper quick to flare these days. I sighed in frustration as I looked down, noticing the dusty trail of footprints I was leaving as I walked through the kitchen. Ever since the fire, they'd been working on rebuilding and the unbearable mess was everywhere.

At the next knock, I looked toward Johnny's bedroom, relieved to see that he was still asleep despite the constant noise. It was eleven a.m., but around our house that seemed more like seven lately, the hours and minutes and days all blurring into one. I opened the door in one fell swoop, like a magician pulling back the curtain on his act, to see a surprisingly tall man standing outside, his hands half pushed into his pockets as he smiled openly at me. He was extremely handsome, with his deep, inviting eyes and straight-lined jaw, and I was suddenly very aware that I didn't have on even a touch of makeup. I glanced at the floor, then back up at his eyes, feeling self-conscious and ridiculous in my bare feet and morning hair, fighting the urge to close the door rudely without another word out of embarrassment.

Despite being tall myself, over 5'10, he made me feel small, even dainty, and I realized while trying to suppress a grin that I liked it. He was at least six inches taller than I was, maybe more. Subconsciously, I glanced toward his wedding ring finger to find it empty before chiding myself, alarmed at my own spastic mind. *Why would it even matter?* I wondered indignantly, reprimanding myself.

"Julia," he said with candor, his strong voice full of implication and integrity, taking me instantly aback. He obviously knew me, or at least my name, though for the life of me, I didn't know how. I stepped onto the wraparound, creaking front porch, letting the screen door swing shut behind me. I could see this was going to take a while and I certainly didn't want to wake up granddaddy, hoping like me, Elsie was meeting him in the soft place of his dreams. I looked at the stranger with confused, squinting eyes, trying again to place him, to solve the mystery of his presence. He seemed familiar yet new at the same time, and just the sound of his voice produced something akin to inspiration inside of me, evoking long-forgotten desires and thoughts, almost frightening me at their intensity. I watched as the square line of his jaw clenched and his huge, mammoth hands drew my eyes appreciatively as he removed them from his jean pockets. I felt inexplicably emotional, something inside me rapidly weakening at the sight.

When his dark, steady eyes looked into mine directly, their serious brooding was entrancing, and I found it hard to speak. "Do we... know each other?" I asked, my own voice sounding contemplative and foreign, even to my own ears, though I already knew the answer. *Trust me*, I thought, looking at his enchanting chocolate eyes again, *I would have remembered.*

He smiled at me sheepishly; an odd thing, I thought, for a giant of a man like him. I remembered how Elsie had always said, "a gentle man is the only real man" and felt like laughing and crying at the exact same time. His shoulders were expansively broad, like those of a former football player, and as he moved, I saw the muscles flex beneath his shirt, the lean contractions of the curves making me stare. Grabbing a post on the porch, I suddenly felt the need to lean on it, my legs weak and trembling as if I'd just finished working out. "I was here the night of the fire," he said, his immense, ample shoulders now making sense. "I'm sorry," he said apologetically, looking at the porch floor almost as if he were embarrassed, "I thought you might recognize me. I was one of the firefighters."

I smiled at him widely, relieved to place him, trying to stop my shaking knees. "Oh... now it makes sense. I thought I knew you from somewhere." He grinned at me, almost as if he were amused but trying to hide it, and again I felt subtly self-conscious, my one arm crossing over my body and holding the other awkwardly. "You know, your eye really has healed well," he said, his eyes dancing and full of fireworks. "I mean, it only took fifteen years."

I stared at him until I thought I might burn a hole right through him, convinced I was still in my bed, that this was all a dream, that it couldn't really be him, here, on this porch, with me. I felt my face soften like a changed heart as my voice lost most of its strength.

"Dawson?" I asked quietly, never taking my hopeful, delighted eyes from his. He smiled dreamily, and the next thing I knew, I was in the inviting, warm arms of the little boy who had given me a black eye so many years ago, only now, he was all grown up.

"Dawson," I whispered again, feeling every sensation, my voice thicker with raw emotion than I expected. "You came back," I said, astonished, longing to hold him forever. He touched my face with his smooth, leather hand, briefly stroking it in small, circular motions. It was remarkably strong and decisively gentle at the same time, more delicate than its size let on. "I had to," he said honestly, looking at me with a kind of tenderness I had never seen before as he held my face in his hands, warming me like a burst of fresh sunlight.

"Something was missing," he told me, stripping back the hard layers inside of me one by one, exposing my vulnerability, cropping up into my heart like a rose among thorns, bringing beauty back into my life. As I looked at him lovingly, I felt my heart clench just like it had five years ago, in a different lifetime, on the day of our high school graduation. "It was you," he said.

Return

J essica was sitting across from me in a padded, mahogany colored corner booth that was faded from the sun as we ate lunch at a local waterfront restaurant downtown, the bay picture window giving way to an incredible view of a docked sailboat on the water. She looked at me as I spoke, her violet eyes as wide as saucers, revealing her unmasked surprise. "Are you *kidding* me?" she asked and I couldn't help but to laugh in reply at her expression.

"No, Jess, he really came back!" I laughed. "We talked for hours on my porch yesterday. He told me how he had gone to USC for undergrad, gotten his degree, and was on track to be a lawyer at his father's firm when he changed his mind," I explained, the words still feeling like a dream as I spoke them.

"He decided he wants to help people, to help our community specifically, so he became a firefighter over in Summerville. That's what he had been doing for the past year, and of course he dated other people, and so did I as you know, but he told me that no matter who he was with, I was always in the back of his mind... that I always had been. That is why he decided to come back after seeing me the night of the fire...because he knew that we could have something great, despite the way things had ended between us before. After hearing about what happened with Lincoln, he finally understood."

She shook her head and smiled at me astonishingly, amazed at how the sequence of events had unfolded like a storyline right before her. "I knew it," she said smugly, leaning against the back of the booth and silently congratulating herself on her strong sense of intuition, staring at me.

"Knew what?" I asked, laughing back, her behavior cracking me up in every way.

"You and Dawson!" she replied before I finished my question, almost spitting the words out as she spoke them. "You two have been crazy about each other ever since we were kids and we all knew you two would end up together. I think everyone knew it except for you!" I took a huge bite of my freshly made, delicious yeast roll and downed a big gulp of my sweet tea with its extra fined crushed ice.

"Seriously?" I asked, doubt crossing my features like a shadow. Now it was her turn to laugh at me.

"I cannot believe you didn't know, Julia! I knew, he knew... girl, we all knew!" she said again, giggling, digging into her Cobb salad, taking a bite of the blue cheese and tomatoes while I responded.

"Well," I said, smiling at my own naivety of the past. "Better late than never, right?" I quipped back smugly, scrunching up my nose at Jessica playfully.

She laughed at my ridiculousness, jokingly rolling her eyes. "Yeah, I suppose you are right," she said, turning serious again, taking a big, hungry bite of her salad. "So did you completely freak out when you realized it was him?"

I saw my opening and took it, giving Jessica all the details of the early morning hair, his big hands, and the way his eyes captured something inside me that I still couldn't explain. Her face grew with excitement as I spoke, watching as my eyes lit up with happiness.

"Julia," she said reflectively, "this guy could be your Noah." I chuckled as I remembered our many sleepovers as teenagers filled with ice cream, chick flicks, and hopes of our husbands. Who could have known that we would be here now, talking about someone who might *actually* be the one for me? My eyes glazed over in dreams of something rare as our waitress refilled my always-empty glass. "Yeah," I said back distractedly, thoughts of possibility racing through my mind, growing like a blazing wildfire. "You know, he just might be."

Later that same night, Dawson picked me up, around eight. He was wearing dark washed jeans and a striped blue button down long sleeved shirt, with the sleeves rolled up to his elbows. His dark, short hair was gelled slightly and I could smell the faint scent of Hugo Boss cologne as I hugged him, thinking it was the most amazing thing that I had ever smelled. I closed my eyes and breathed it in, enjoying the way it seemed so manly in contrast with the vanilla scented perfume I was wearing.

"You are gorgeous," he whispered, the sound of his voice taking me back, slipping his arm around me while we walked to his car. He opened the door for me and I climbed in, taking a seat comfortably in his silver Honda Civic. He walked over to the other side of the car and climbed into the driver's side seat, taking hold of the wheel, his large hands making it seem as if it belonged on a model car instead of a real one. Then, as if he remembered something important, he let go of the wheel and turned to me.

"Do you mind being blindfolded?" he asked, holding up a silk black scarf. I laughed as I looked at it, thinking it seemed so womanly against those big, rugged hands.

"As long as you promise to never wear it," I joked, laughing at him.

"Oh, don't worry," he chuckled along with me. "I just bought it for tonight."

That made me smile and I turned towards the passenger window so he could tie it loosely around my eyes, fully trusting him. This was Dawson, after all. I waited a few moments in the darkness, expecting to feel the car jerk and begin reversing after he changed gears.

"Okay," he said a moment later, sounding relieved though I didn't know why. "What?" I asked, completely confused.

"I've been waving my hand in front of the scarf," he said elusively. "Testing you," he finally admitted with goodwill. "Now I know you are as blind as a bat."

I reached over with my tiny arm and touched him, playfully smacking his chest. "I have my eyes closed, crazy person!" As we both laughed at one another and the fun we were having, I felt the car pull into reverse and ease out of the driveway as we began to head out for a night of surprise.

I knew it had to be only minutes that we were driving, but it seemed much longer, the blindfold distorting my senses and blending things together. I could feel every move the car made, hear the roar and acceleration of the engine, and feel the cool night breeze coming in from the sunroof above us. "Are you too cold, Julia?" Dawson asked me kindly as we drove along and I half-smiled to myself at the words, remembering a different boy years ago who didn't care at all.

"It feels great," I reassured Dawson and he agreed, holding my left hand the entire time he drove, its inherent heat soothing me at its touch. Eventually, I felt the car coming to a steady slowdown and braced myself, wondering where we could be and thinking how exciting it all was, feeling the sensation pulsing through my veins and overwhelming me. He led me out of the car and across what felt like pea gravel and hard, packed dirt, steadying and stabilizing me as I climbed up something I couldn't see, until I reached the top and he eventually helped me to sit down, feeling the cold, metal surface just beneath me.

"Are you okay?" he asked before letting go of my hand. I nodded alertly, feeling alive, and he removed the blindfold.

When I opened my eyes, I saw what I never expected, the memories washing me away, crashing over me like a flood. Above me, the stars were abundant, and the sky was a deep, brooding shade of black, filled with mystery and wonder. A few clouds were scattered overhead, remnants of the long day, their dark silver lining creating an ethereal effect. Pink and red rose petals covered the ground in a broad pattern that encircled us while tall candles illuminated the night, weaving in and out of the petals that covered the ground. All around us, fireflies danced on the warm evening breeze, their lovely glow painting the sky with gorgeousness.

Dawson was sitting beside me, watching my every starstruck reaction. It took me a moment to finally realize where I was; the thought of returning here again had never crossed my mind. It had been so long, fifteen years I suddenly realized with surprise. "I wanted you to have a good memory of us here, Julia," he whispered, placing a piece of hair that had fallen out behind my ear again, his touch sending a heavenly tingle down my spine.

He leaned in sweetly and kissed me, a kiss I now realized I had waited for my entire life. "I love you, Julia," he whispered, his words reflecting my heart. "I always have." As I looked at Dawson and the moon bathed us in its warm night glow, I felt the emotions inside of me start to swell and I began, for the second time in my life, to cry on that ancient old jungle gym. Only this time, they were the happiest tears I could have ever imagined. "I love you too, Dawson," I breathed, the celestial stars twinkling brightly overhead, God's finger-painting of approval.

Wind

The next year with Dawson passed quickly, my world feeling full of promise and better days, like the first breath of a brand new year. It felt as if we had been waiting our whole lives to explore what might happen between us and now that we'd captured it, we were both reluctant at the thought of ever letting it go. After he returned to town, things seemed to fall into place so naturally and we established a pattern of normalcy as most couples do. We were getting to know each other as adults, yes, but there was so much between us that we already knew, that was already understood, like reconnecting with an old best friend after years apart.

Dawson and I went everywhere together, not able to stand being apart for very long, like two halves of one loudly beating heart. We ventured to church services every week, tried new types of food for dinner at least a few times a month, laughed uncontrollably at the new comedy movies playing at the theater up the road, visited parks and plantations, even cemeteries, and often, went on more wonderful, captivating surprise dates.

Once he took me to Cypress Gardens and rowed me on the lake where Noah took Allie in *The Notebook* and I almost died from the romance of it all, the gigantic cypress trees surrounding us like a sweeping canopy. The next week, I took him deep sea fishing on the Atlantic and we caught a twenty-three-pound silver tarpon and from Dawson's face, I think that summed up his idea of romance pretty well, too. There was laughter and tears and happiness and silence and a perfect mixture of all that made a relationship brim with life and passion.

Sometimes, Dawson would just come to our simple, humble house and sit with granddaddy and me as Johnny recounted his stories from the war of saving and of being saved countless times by his fellow comrades, of their haunting talks in smoky mud pits as the bombs exploded around them and resounded in their ears, ringing loudly. Other times, we would play games with feigned competitiveness, *Apples to Apples* and *UNO* among our favorites, and although Johnny denied it slyly, even now we all knew he tried to let me win to this day.

Dawson and I would share stories and memories of people we grew up with, even of the triplet girls who'd grown up and attended Harvard. Two of them had at least; little Savannah Hampton had lost her life when she was only nineteen, texting and driving without a seatbelt when she was hit by a drunk driver just three minutes from home and expelled from her seat. She crashed hard on the pavement, her perfect blue eyes closing forever and meeting the sweetness of eternity in a flash. Life really was just a held-out breath, a glimpse into forever, and then, without warning, it was gone.

We talked about Lincoln, the murmurs we'd heard from our friends throughout the years about his time in the Coast Guard after getting his GED, welcome whispers of a life well lived. Always, we would listen to Johnny talk about life with a wisdom we would never forget, one that imprinted itself on our hearts in an immovable way.

Many times, Johnny drifted off to sleep in his Lazy-Boy, lured by Elsie's famed lullabies from the sky, at least I liked to imagine so. Dawson and I would sneak off to cuddle and kiss on the porch swing when the night outside was still and soft, the crickets and bullfrogs keeping us company with soothing lullabies of their own. There was no need for words as we listened to the rhythmic, natural creaking of the swing as our feet guided it back and forth in a steady rhythm.

Other times we would talk until early in the morning, when the majestic sun would just begin to peek over the edge of the horizon. In those moments, we would marvel at how our easy conversation made the hours fly by and the comfort that we had with one another, as if we'd never been apart at all. Our bond was built not only in our lives as adults, but was one that had blossomed within the growth of our youth, a full circle of compatibility.

In so many ways I still could not believe he was here, with his ability to bring me to roaring levels of laughter, with his level-headed approach to life, with his smart, inventive, hardworking ways, with his unmatched character and love for the Lord. Even more so than that, I was so indescribably thankful that *we* were here. Deep down I had always known I wanted to be with Dawson, but when he left after graduation, I figured we didn't have a chance considering what happened and simply gave up. During college, we were both dating other people and it seemed that we never had our moment, always being with someone else.

Now, as he held me in his brawny arms and gently whispered his love for me, I realized that we might not have been ready before; maybe we would have been too young and immature, ruining what was meant to be.

I heard Granny's words ringing in my memory: '*You have to remem-*

ber your dreams. One day you will look up, and he will be there. God's providence is always perfect.'

"Thank you," I whispered into the gusty, open night, though my voice was so quiet that the wind blew it away.

Angel Oak

"**D**awson, look at this picture." I said, handing him the old, ancient black and white photograph that I was cradling in my hand. "Can you believe this?"

"Where in the world are they?" He mused aloud, looking at the immense, towering tree surrounding Johnny and Elsie.

"It has to be the Angel Oak," I said assuredly, leaning over his wide shoulders and looking down at the photo again. "It's the only one that big!" His eyes were fixated, glued on the intricate, knotted branches and roots that intertwined in one another like an interlocking puzzle.

"Why is it so gigantic? I didn't even know they had trees like this. Look at the roots, Jul."

"I know." I looked at the photo, thinking of the centuries of ancient history behind it. "Have you never heard the story?"

He laughed, moving closer to me with a playful, unexpected kiss. "Obviously not," I giggled, smiling back, wrapping my arms around his strong neck, feeling like I was holding my whole heart.

Dawson's face abruptly changed and it made me stop laughing immediately. Broken beams of sunshine flowed in from the window nearby, warming us both upon their impact. By the light of their hazy glow, I saw Johnny's tired frame entering the room, the smell of his Old Spice cologne hanging thickly in the air as he did.

"Hey Granddaddy," I said, putting the photograph down on the chipped, brown coffee table in front of us. "Are you feeling okay to-day?"

He hadn't been out of his room yet, though it was almost four p.m. now. I had peeked in a few times, but he had been deep in sleep or sitting by the open window, looking through an old box I had never seen before, lost in another world. I didn't know whether or not to ask so I'd just kissed his cheek and let him be, not wanting to pretend to understand everything he was going through.

I knew it had to be hard for him, to be in the same house, the same room where so many things had happened that reminded him of Elsie, to see the countless quilts she'd made by hand, still smell the scent of her lingering like a wish on the pillow he slept beside every night. He had tragically lost his wife, but the house, for the most part, had survived. It seemed oddly cruel when I thought about it for too long and I made myself stop, feeling bitterness waiting at the door.

Johnny was dressed like the sweet old man he was, in high-waisted black pants, black socks, and a gray argyle sweater. He looked inde-scribably adorable, but I worried that he might be cold as he usually was these days, a constant, bone deep chill seeming to almost come from within.

"Let me get your slippers." I instructed, quickly moving from the couch and toward the bedroom to retrieve them.

"No, no." He slowly shuffled to the couch with tiny, shaky steps, his ragged breathing making me worry and I flinched a little as I watched him. Dawson had moved so that Johnny could sit beside me, a wide opening now between us. "I feel okay."

Dawson patted the empty space by him on the couch, inviting granddaddy in. "Now... what were you two saying about the tree?"

I looked at Dawson with an expression of regret, the pang of making a mistake feeling fresh. It was too soon. I shouldn't have had the pictures out yet. "It's nothing, Granddaddy. We were just looking at some old pictures."

I reached for the photo box to put it away, but his deep, quiet voice gave me pause. "Please don't," he whispered, his eyes pleading for a reason that I didn't understand. I looked at Dawson again, unsure as to what I should do.

"Okay," I said, but didn't move, shooting Dawson another concerned look instead.

He held out his hands patiently. "Can I see it?"

"Of course, Granddaddy, it's yours." I handed it over tentatively, watching him closely. His eyes lit up, but then they began to water and I snapped into action at the sight.

"Oh, no," I lunged for the photo box again, but he reached for me tenderly, cupping my anxious hands, his mild manner stopping me in my tracks. "It's okay, Julia. The older you grow, the more you will begin to understand me. Tears are beautiful; they are how you let the pain in your heart drip out. It's a good thing, not to hold it all inside."

I looked at him with awe and protection in the same moment; feeling as if I was his child and his mother almost in one instant. He needed me, I knew, but I also needed him. He was teaching me every moment. "You're right, Granddaddy," I conceded, leaning back against the couch, resigning myself to his wisdom.

"I could hear a little from the other room," he started, looking at Dawson for support. "I wanted to tell you the story. Of the tree," He pointed to the picture that laid loosely on the table, beckoning to me like a haunting dream. "And of us." Johnny looked at me, catching my scanning eyes and settling them. "There were a lot of things that happened that you don't know yet either," he said, surprising me in every way. Dawson and I were both looking directly at him, anticipation hanging thick in the air like a gust of clouds.

"The tree itself," he informed, "is the oldest living thing this side of the Rockies. It is 1,500 years old if you can believe it. That means it was here hundreds of years before Columbus was in the New World." We both looked on with big eyes; surprised anything could live to be that old in this society.

"But that is only the history, of course." He cleared his throat as if preparing for an announcement. "The real story, to me, is the one that began in 1946. Julia, do you remember when I told you that Elsie and I met on the sidewalk outside of this house?" I easily nodded yes, a lump forming in my throat at the memory. "Of course I do," I whispered, pushing it down.

"I met Elsie on the day that they first placed the concrete in front of our houses. She lived next door to me, and when they had finished pouring the sidewalk and left it to dry, I found my curiosity running wild. I had never seen it before and had to get an up close look."

"Well, it turns out that Elsie had that same sense of curiosity as I did and I met her in front of my house looking down at the drying pavement, a little girl with two pink bows in her hair. Even though we had just met we decided that we would put our initials in the cement before it dried. For whatever reason, it just seemed like something we should do." He smiled at the memory, lost happily in the past.

"To this day they are still there, sixty-four years later. We were just a couple of crazy kids, looking for an adventure." He exhaled to himself, a look of satisfaction crossing his face, as if he'd just found the secret of the stars.

"Of course, I didn't know at six years old on a slab of drying cement that I had just met my wife, but as the years went on I quickly learned that I had begun the best adventure of my life at that exact moment." I was on the verge of crying as he went on, every word playing out as a movie in my mind.

"The sidewalk, if you followed it long enough, led right to the Angel Oak Tree. Not many people knew about it then, as it was far off in a patch of woods, but we did. We were always seeking out new adventures since the first day we met and we ran across that ancient old oak tree one day. We'd spend hours and hours on it, playing hide and seek or seeing who could climb the branches the highest before chickening out. One time I even fell and broke my arm trying to beat her to the top." He laughed a little, studying the photograph, his eyes so full of love.

"As the tree grew older, so did we and everything seemed to change in life as it always does. But through the years, two things never did change and that was our love for each other and the old oak tree. It was always there. It was able to withstand so many things through-out the years: hurricanes, floods, even earthquakes. It continued to flourish, no matter what the circumstances were... that is always how we felt about our love. Times were not always easy, but it continued to grow and get stronger and so did we." I was listening intently, hanging on his every word, mesmerized by the account of a love so rare.

"I had my first date gazing at the stars with Elsie under that tree, I kissed her for the first time there, and later in life I asked her to marry me under it in the middle of spring. The tree was in full bloom and it seemed as though there were hundreds of branches going everywhere, with her favorite flower growing as far as you could see in every direction. It was the most beautiful thing I had ever seen." He paused, resting in a time so long ago, still feeling her in every breath he inhaled. "She was the most beautiful woman I had ever seen."

Johnny handed Dawson the photo and he studied it for a long time before handing it to me. I could see the wild roses blooming in every direction, just as he had described, enchanted that it was a true story, their story, which to me had already been so captivating. I looked at Johnny with amazement, shaking my head from side to side in disbelief. "Why didn't you ever tell me this?" I questioned, slightly put off at the realization.

"Oh," he laughed kindly, touching my arm. "Don't be hurt, sweetheart. A husband and a wife always keep secrets together, something special hidden away from the world. This was nothing different."

I felt as if I had peeked in on a private moment, one that I was not meant to see. "Oh," I set the photo down and pushed it away, the sudden sting of intrusion flooding my depths. "Well, I hope she wouldn't mind you telling me."

Johnny watched me carefully, physically seeing my uneasiness on display as I fidgeted. "Julia," he coaxed, turning the picture back over and pushing it toward me again. "It's just the opposite. I know that she would want me to tell you now, in this way, when you can appreciate it the most." He looked from Dawson to me and back again, obviously loving us, treating us both like his children. "We thought about telling you when you were younger, but you're older now. You are in love. It means more," he said and like stone rolling away from a tomb, I felt my heart open up.

I looked at him with kind eyes, knowing he was right, thinking he always could peer into my soul like glass. "Are you always trying to teach me something?" I jokingly asked, blushing at my overreaction.

"Are you always looking for something to learn?" he countered, his eyes unburdened for the first time in months, the rays of light suddenly filling them with splendid abandon.

Rubies

T he next morning I found Johnny sitting by the open window again, the fresh air pouring into the room like a melody. He was looking at the secret box, carefully going through its contents, this time long before dawn. I was on my way to the kitchen for a glass of water when I saw him, having woken up thirsty and trudging to the kitchen for some relief. I stopped at his door when I saw his light on, peeking through the open crack, unsure as to whether or not I should let my presence be known.

I heard him speaking to God as though he was talking with a friend, telling him of his deep grief and that he wasn't sure if he could go on. He was praying that the Lord would make his time to go home soon, saying that he wanted to go. Johnny asked that God would take care of me as He always had, especially after he died. I felt like my heart had literally broken apart inside of my chest. I knew this moment wasn't meant for my ears.

I walked into the kitchen and began to quietly pull a glass from the dishwasher. I filled it with water and quickly downed it followed by three more. I tried to calm my breathing, shaken up by even the mere thought of losing Johnny.

I had been so worried about taking care of him that the pain of losing Elsie was still strong, but somehow manageable because I had someone else who needed me. I cried when I needed to, but I stayed strong for Johnny as much as I could. When I do lose him, though, I know I won't be able to be strong anymore in that moment. I kept refilling my glass and gulping down what seemed to be gallons of water when I suddenly heard his steady shuffle coming my way and shut the faucet off. I felt so selfish for disturbing his prayers over a glass of water.

"Hi Julia," he said, his old voice hoarse and low, deeper than normal due to the hour. "What are you doing up so early?"

I pointed to my eighty-seventh glass. "Thirsty."

His tired eyes crinkled as he smiled. "So I heard," he said, pointing to the water tap. I cringed at his words.

"I have something I want you to look at," he said, time moving slowly in the simple kitchen, shrouded by the dark night. "I've been working on it ever since Elsie...ever since she went home. The funeral home told me that I needed to tell them the inscription for her gravestone by this morning. I've been thinking about it constantly, but nothing seemed good enough."

"I read all the cliché sayings, wrote some things of my own... but how can you describe someone like her? It would be easier to tell a blind man what the sunrise is like at the first dawn of morning. I've been trying for days, years really, without ever finding the words."

The same words coming out of anyone else's mouth might've sounded false, but not here, not from this man who'd spent his whole life devotedly loving one woman more than most could even imagine.

I nodded, looking at the paper he was grasping in his hands, wondering desperately what he had written on it. "I finally thought of the best thing, I hope. I think she would really be proud to know it is true." He extended it towards me and I took it into my hands timidly.

"I was hoping you might be the first to see it," he whispered, clutching the edge of a chair for stability. He looked away, the pain evident. I turned the paper over and read the words in front of me. I felt my hand cover my mouth instinctively as I saw what was scrawled in tiny block letters on the tear- stained page:

PROVERBS 31:10

"A VIRTUOUS WOMAN WHO CAN FIND?
FOR HER PRICE IS FAR ABOVE RUBIES."

I FOUND HER.

"She would love it," I choked out, wiping my blurry, shimmering eyes. "It's the most beautiful thing I've ever seen."

Storybook

On the morning of our one-year anniversary, I woke up early to the ringing of the doorbell. Rolling out of bed, I laughed instantly, thinking that if it were Dawson, at least it wouldn't be the first time he had seen me with no makeup on. I rushed to answer it, my bare feet pitter-pattering across the hardwood floors, but when I opened the door and looked around expectantly, oddly, no one was there.

Feeling confused, I stepped outside, the screen door slamming shut behind me as it always did, and looked onto the porch. Sitting alone on the white porch swing, the one where I'd sat with Dawson and talked for hours the first morning when he came back, I saw a black garment bag zipped up with a single white rose laying on it and rushed over, wanting to examine it more closely. When I did, I saw a hand scrawled note that said in clearly male penmanship, "*Wear me tonight at five p.m., my love."* I giggled with a surge of excitement and ran back inside the house to try it on. "Granddaddy, look at this!" I squeaked, delighted.

The dress was absolutely breathtaking. It was a light peach maxi dress made of a luxurious chiffon material, with a silk black ribbon wrapping around the front, giving the baby doll style dress a personal touch of my favorite go-to color. It fit perfectly, almost as though it were made for me alone. The dress landed a few inches below my knees and hung loosely with my body's natural curves, modestly accentuating all the right places. It had a square neckline that touched my collarbone and medium sized tank straps that held it up on each shoulder. It was completely beautiful and perfect, the kind of dress I could wear on our anniversary or even to a fancy occasion at church and I absolutely adored it already.

Johnny made no point of hiding his exuberant happiness as he watched me fix my hair, put on makeup, and spend an unnaturally long time in the bathroom getting ready, primping to make sure every detail was just right. When five p.m. arrived, I had my brown locks straightened and flowing halfway down my back while my makeup remained subtle yet alluring.

On top of my normal routine, I had added a touch of all over bronzer on my high cheekbones, outlined the rims of my eyes with soft black eyeliner, and used smooth green eye shadow that made my dark brown eyes pop. "Oh, Julia," granddaddy whispered when he saw me, choking up a little, like a proud daddy greeting his daughter on her wedding day. "You look stunning." I hugged him tightly before heading out the door, slipping my white heels onto my feet easily on my way. "I love you," I told him genuinely, waving goodbye as I left.

When I stepped outside expecting to see the Honda driving up, I felt my mouth fall open in shock when I saw a horse drawn carriage pulled up along the street's edge, waiting on me. Dawson was standing just outside my front door, dressed in a full black suit with a silky bright blue tie. "Ready, baby?" he asked sweetly, taking my hand and walking me to the carriage, which was led by a proud brown horse, and as it began to pull away, I looked back and saw Johnny standing at the window peering out, smiling as if he knew something that I didn't.

Our first stop of the night was at my favorite restaurant, Marten Elli's, a fantastic Italian place where the only thing better than the food was the service, making us feel as if we were the only people there. Dawson was a true gentleman, coming around to my side and opening my door, carefully helping me down from the carriage, and I saw other women outside the restaurant looking my way in envy.

Inside, I ordered a bowl of the world's best macaroni and cheese, always a kid at heart, while Dawson got the fettuccine alfredo and a caesar side salad with extra croutons. For dessert, we split a huge piece of chocolate cheesecake with fresh strawberries and raspberry drizzle, all of it indescribably delicious. The atmosphere was magical as low-lit lights dimmed the room while a private cello player performed classical music in the background, music we both so loved, Bach's Cello Suite Number 1 in G Major being my absolute favorite of the night. "This is wonderful," I said breathlessly, taken by the perfect, storybook evening of surprises he had planned, the romance of all it overtaking me.

"There's more," he whispered, meeting my eyes with excitement. My expression grew larger as if to ask what it was, but he shook his head and smiled, refusing my curiosity. "Just a little while longer," he said playfully, torturing me to make it more fun. I bit the edge of my lip, feigning frustration but secretly thrilled, enjoying the night of continuing surprises.

After dinner, I saw the familiar silky black blindfold I had met on the night of the jungle gym and immediately laughed as he fastened it with ease and the carriage took us to our next destination. I could hear the loud rumbling from a distance off and began to wonder where in the world he was taking me. "Dawson," I laughed, trying to pry something out of him, but he wouldn't budge even a little. He hugged me tightly and I could feel his heartbeat thumping against me like a hummingbird's wings, flittering with excitement. "Just wait," he instructed, the quick response in his voice giving away his level of enthusiasm.

Moments later, I felt the pull of the reins and the horses came to a slow trot as the carriage began to stop. "Now," he whispered, removing the blindfold as I opened my anxious eyes, "Happy Anniversary." Directly in front of us was a massive, hot air balloon ready to launch, its colors reminding me of the wings of a butterfly and I covered my mouth in surprise, looking at him in shock. "Dawson, are you serious?" I whispered, clinging to his hand tightly and giggling, feeling like we were kids again.

"Of course I am," he replied, taking my hand and leading me to the huge balloon. "I know you always wanted to know what it would feel like to fly." I smiled so big at his words, my heart inflating, loving that he listened to me, that he remembered the littlest things I'd say, but even forget myself. He was incredibly thoughtful and it was so attractive. Once inside the balloon, it began rapidly to ascend higher and higher, and though my fear of heights made my stomach turn and do flips, I soon learned to let go and enjoy the moment. It was amazingly quiet, so undisturbed and peaceful, that I felt like the whole world was taking a single, silent breath at the same time, as if the heart of the earth had paused just for us.

Dawson stood behind me, holding me with his chin on my shoulder, his stubble arousing something wild and free in me, as we sailed far above the ocean, the view so extreme and extraordinary that it left me simply awed. The sun had begun to set over the water, its colors a whirlwind of deep purples, pinks, and shaded blues, its reflection catching at moments over the glistening waves and reflecting its light. I gasped responsively as I looked below us and saw two dolphins midair, their slick, silver grey bodies moving in conjunction with the unpredictable motion of the late afternoon waves. The world laid open before us in every direction: the people on the shore were as tiny as specks, no hotels or high-rises in sight, only uncaptured beauty and perfect calm all around. Dawson kissed my check tenderly before turning me around to face him and as I looked into his soft, puppy dog eyes, I saw everything I ever wanted in this world.

"Julia," he said, still entrancing me with his deep brown stare. "I have been praying for you ever since I can remember. I have always loved you and I always will." His gentle words seeped into my soul and I felt my heart take flight. Dawson dropped to one knee and smiled at me, beaming with joy, as my eyes filled with up with happy tears. "Will you give me the privilege of being my wife?"

He opened the delicate, smooth black ring box and I looked down at a princess cut, one-carat diamond ring, the sunshine catching its every intricate sparkle. Even with the clear blue ocean, the smoldering sunset, and the endlessly crashing waves, in that moment all I could look at were Dawson's perfect eyes as I heartily whispered a "Yes."

Coffee

Johnny was lying in a cold, rigid hospital bed, barely conscious, waiting for a nurse to give him his pills. When I arrived home from my date last night, I strolled in the door smiling and already talking away, only to find him lying on the floor, sprawled helplessly across the kitchen, with a broken cup of piping hot coffee spilled all over his new pants. I screamed earnestly for help before dialing 911, not knowing how long he had been there, cradling his head in my lap, holding onto my hero and praying he would come back to me. "Granddaddy!" I cried, panic-stricken, feeling like I was dying too.

He was conscious, but barely, and I immediately felt my heart sink back into the night I lost Elsie, the jolting ache of a loss with no warning. It felt close to the same way, but only this time, it was much worse; Johnny was the only family I had left. The paramedics had arrived within minutes and determined that he had suffered a mild stroke before taking him in the ambulance to the hospital. He was disoriented and forgetful, not remembering much, so I couldn't be sure if he had laid there needing me for minutes or hours before I finally found him. I laid my head in my hands and cried, the panic giving way to shameful regret.

"Oh, honey," the nurse said when she saw me from across the room, my frame tiny and shaken, sitting in a weakly padded chair, "He'll be alright now, don't you worry." I appreciated what she was trying to do, but it was still of no comfort, as I knew I should have been there as he had always been there for me, the very first second he needed me. The nurse tried to help Johnny take his pills, but he refused, shaking his head vigorously and turning away, disoriented and stubborn, closing his mouth in protest. The nurse looked at me and smiled, her calming presence and patience impressing me immensely. Her job was no picnic. "Come here, honey," she said kindly, gesturing to me and encouraging me with her sweet voice.

I stood up automatically and walked to his bedside, feeling sleep-deprived and robotic. "Now I'm not supposed to do this," she said, tilting her head to the right, peeking toward the door to find that the hallway was empty of observers. "But I can see that you two have a very special relationship." She handed me the pill, so tiny and powder blue, with numbers etched on it. "Would you like to try?" she nudged and I weakly agreed as she moved aside, the guilt still haunting the back of my mind.

"Granddaddy," I coaxed gently, hoping he would listen and know it was me. "It's Julia." His eyes looked at me blankly, foggy from his earlier dosage, before registering slight recognition when he stared into my dark brown eyes, seeing a reflection of his own. "I'm going to give you this little pill now, okay? It's going to help you feel better."

He didn't nod, but when I placed the pill in his mouth he swallowed it down quickly, allowing me to help with his water, and the action alone made me want to cry. It all felt so final, so devastatingly sad. "Good," I assured, patting him. "Now you should feel better soon." Sitting beside him, I reached for his hand, covered with taped on tubes, then turned to look at the nurse and she smiled an affected smile at me. "Thank you," I spoke, speaking to both her and to God, and she nodded. I wondered how many thank you's she got a day, and somehow felt that it probably wasn't enough. To me, she was admirable beyond description, a heroine even.

"He can't talk very much right now, but he can hear you," she said, heading for the door, giving us the privacy we needed. "Sometimes it helps them," she commented while looking down, jotting notes on her clipboard, before starting to walk out. "And you," she added gently, meeting my gaze for a moment before disappearing altogether.

I breathed a slow, unsteady breath out, not knowing if I could do this, not thinking I held the kind of strength a moment like this needed. It took a couple of moments to compose myself, but I tried to be strong for granddaddy, telling him all about the engagement and the way that Dawson had surprised me, every last heartwarming, unexpected detail. "He's coming by to visit you as soon as he gets off work today," I mentioned, knowing Johnny must be missing him too. They were so close.

Then, I thought I saw something out of the corner of my eye, though I couldn't be sure. Maybe I was delirious from the lack of sleep, or maybe I was just plain seeing things, but no matter what the reason, I thought I saw Johnny give a little smile at the edges of his mouth, his subtle stamp of approval, when I told him that I had said, "Yes."

Rose Petals

Dawson had been so understanding about my need to move the wedding up, and about all my concerns over granddaddy's health. It had always been my dream as his little girl that he would walk me down the aisle, and the thought of him not being a part of my wedding reduced me to ashes. On the night of our engagement, Dawson and I had made tentative plans for when we might have the wedding, deciding that at Middleton Place, on an arched white bridge, overlooking the still creek water, next April when the camellias are in bloom would be lovely, roughly giving us a year to plan it all.

When he arrived at the hospital the night after Johnny's accident with Chick-Fil-A in tow, we'd discussed it more after finishing up dinner, as Johnny slept sweetly and his snores filled the air every now and again. "Dawson, I want to move the wedding up. I need granddaddy to be there to walk me down the aisle."

He shook his head, completely agreeing that things had changed and we had more important considerations now than flowers. "I know," he added, taking my hand in his own. "I want him there too. I just can't imagine it without him. So how soon are we talking?" he asked curiously, wondering if we could really pull it off.

I looked at him seriously, half-biting my lip in anxiety. "How about this Saturday?" I asked, wide-eyed and desperately hopeful against all odds that we could make it work. Dawson looked at my face for one long moment before shaking his head, rubbing my hand as he held it tightly. "I think Saturday would be perfect, babe."

Two days later, on Thursday morning, after choking down half a hospital banana and a third of a glass of water, they released Johnny from the hospital, escorting him out to the car in a wheelchair he despised. He made the best of it, though, joking about trying to pop a few wheelies and getting back to his normal self, showing the humorous side I so loved. I was determined to never leave him again, at least for a while, and Dawson, being the nearly perfect man that he was, volunteered to handle all the arrangements.

"Are you sure?" I asked, astonished at the amount of work he was taking on. "Yes, baby," he assured me, squeezing me tightly in a hug, making me smile, something that was tough the last few days. "Is there anything special you want?" he inquired of me. *What in the world did I ever do to deserve a man like him?* I wondered, shaking my head slightly. "As long as I get to marry you and granddaddy walks me down the aisle," I told him, breathing out a sigh of relief at the thought, "That's plenty special enough. I really don't care about the specifics; we can go to the courthouse if we have to. Whatever you do will be absolutely wonderful. Thank you so much, babe." I kissed him firmly then, savoring the fresh sensation of his mouth, his steamy lips slipping into my heart and igniting all my senses, making me feel truly alive for the first time since he'd last left my side.

When Saturday morning came, Johnny was fragile and exhausted, still needing long periods of quiet rest and assistance with almost everything, but he was mobile enough. I was thankful because for the past few days, I wasn't sure that he would be. A lot of diligent prayers by the members of our church had been given on his behalf and in this moment, I knew with all certainty they had been answered by God Himself. What I was going to do with all those casseroles, though, I still didn't know. Dawson left a piece of lined notebook paper with all the wedding details scribbled down in his handwriting, taped to the front door on the morning of the wedding, unwilling to risk accidentally seeing me before the ceremony.

The only thing that I selected for the wedding was my dress: a classically white, beautifully simple one with a pickup style bottom, the clear sleeves trailing with beads and falling slightly off the shoulder, topping it all off with a transparent veil scattered with even, small pearls. I wore timeless jewelry, just studded pearl earrings with a single diamond at the top of each and a strand of matching pearls. A shining tiara with a mixture of small beads and diamonds complimented the up do hairstyle I had decided on, wonderfully completing the outfit. I absolutely loved it all and I couldn't wait for Dawson to see it, imaging his face lighting up with pure joy. The note said to arrive promptly at three p.m. for an outdoor wedding at the Angel

Oak Tree, prompting tears from both Johnny and I the moment we read it.

"It's so special," he had whispered, and I hoped that it being there would let Johnny feel honored and not wracked with sorrow at the memories, the flashes of the past ever so close.

Granddaddy seemed excited as we drove to the location, aimlessly drumming his fingertips on his pants and sitting in awe of the sprawling Spanish moss lined drive. The winding roads and flowering plants gave the drive a feel common to the Deep South: that somehow time had stopped and regressed back to the days when things were slower, simpler, somehow. I had always loved the South, filled with its charm and sweet tea, and felt so privileged to have grown up there.

It held a majesty that nowhere else could touch: the people, the food, the accent, the feeling of coming home even if you were visiting for the first time. The road wound around one last, wide corner and we pulled up to the massive tree that Johnny and Elsie had made sacred for me, scenes of their ancient world entering my view.

Directly beneath the tree, there was a white aisle runner with real rose petals scattered all over it, in variations of sweet, creamy white, soft, silvery pink, and faded, dahlia rose red. Looking around with wonder, I noticed next the white wooden chairs sprawling across the lawn facing the old oak tree. Instead of the traditional shape of straight, boxy lines, the chairs had been altered to form the shape of a backwards heart with the tip of it forming where Dawson and I would stand to say our vows.

The timeless tree created a presence I found hard to comprehend in and of itself, like stepping into a fairytale. Decorations of scattered roses had tastefully been added to the branches, their stems tied with silk ribbon to the massive tree limbs, colored in white and pink, equally spaced throughout the branches. It was inspiring and quintessentially Southern in its charm, a wedding like I had never seen before. I smiled broadly as I looked toward the dreamlike scene again with awe, it leaving me soothed and yet breathless, only to realize with gratitude that it was my own.

The ceremony was simple, comfortable and filled with ease, with fewer than 100 guests in attendance. It was lovely and small, decidedly intimate, and held a special meaning knowing that everyone there knew the true importance of this moment. I saw familiar faces I knew from so long ago: former classmates from my school years, close friends of Johnny and Elsie, Jessica standing specially as my maid of honor, and even kind Katie Taylor smiling back at me, her perfect eyes as blue as ever. I looked at the empty seat with a single white rose in it, the one meant to remember Elsie, and felt all the world's emotions in one profound moment.

The music was performed by a live violin quartet and the melodies swelled and fell with bittersweet sounds and feelings, reflecting all of our hearts. As the music came to a peak, Johnny and I peered around the corner, my bouquet filled with flowers from a bright spring day. We were walking slowly, hoping granddaddy could make it, and I felt my breath catch in my throat when I saw Dawson. He was wearing a black, sateen tuxedo with a new white bow tie, looking more handsome than I ever dreamed possible. He smiled at me and I at him, and soon both of our eyes were filled with joyful tears, every single ounce of love we'd ever known pouring out of us in that exact instance as we held one another's eyes.

When we reached the front of the aisle beneath the big limbs of the Angel Oak Tree, the preacher asked, "Who gives this woman to be married to this man?" and granddaddy looked at him with unmasked pride and said, "I do". Then he kissed me goodbye as he gave me away, and in so many ways, I realized I was still his little girl, that I always would be.

The ceremony was tender as we each read vows that we had written to one another, feelings that I almost couldn't find words beautiful enough to express. Dawson's vows began with, "From the moment I first met you, I knew we were two halves of one heart," and I lost it all over again. We exchanged our chosen rings and prayers were offered throughout the ceremony, reminding us of who had brought us together in the first place. Occasionally I would notice the guests when they would smile or laugh as the minister recounted one of our sweet or funny moments, and some began to dab at their eyes with tissues, swept away in the moment, enraptured by the power of our love.

As the ceremony was coming to an end, a large flock of white mourning doves silently made their way toward the Angel Oak Tree, landing on its outstretched branches. A second later, the wind quickly gusted as it picked up speed. Then, in the very moment that we were pronounced husband and wife, Dawson kissed me gently and rose petals began to fall from the sky, as if Heaven had sent them firsthand, the perfect close to this chapter of our forever story.

Memory

It had only been two short months since the wedding and already I was going to lose him. I was sitting at Johnny's bedside, watching the glowing light from his deep brown eyes fade more rapidly with each moment, a dimming candle slowly burning out. I looked at his small, fragile body, a diminutive skeleton now of what it once was, and listened to his shallow, quick breaths as his chest heaved with every effort that he made, a repetitive movement fighting death. After his sudden stroke, Johnny had returned to the doctor's office for a checkup just two weeks later, and it was then they had found the cancerous tumors growing like thistles among wildflowers, substantial and encroaching on his life and his lungs.

My mind wandered helplessly and I dazed out at the memory, wondering how anyone deals with such a fate as his; how is it even remotely possible? I knew that with Johnny it was about his faith in

God; it was always about his faith in God, every fleeting moment, every cranny of his existence; that alone would carry him through. His days now felt numbered in a very real, tangible sense, not in a distant way like a far off, blazing sunset, seen but never close enough to touch, to realistically comprehend. Every day, he knew, and I knew, could be his last. The pang in my heart at the thought was certain and fierce, gripping me and destroying me in one breath.

I thought of the solitary, dismayed man sitting on the cracked pavement by my side when Elsie died, the one in front of the smoldering flames of a life lost, and how I thought he had looked so different from the man I first met as a little girl. The fire seemed as if it were a lifetime ago and the man beside me now, the one whose bedside I was at, was so different than the man I saw even then. He was so frail, so weak, and so helpless that it seemed as if he were a child now instead of the one who had always taken care of me. As I looked at him and remembered the strong, gentle way he'd rocked me on his knees and whispered lullabies when I was a child, I felt my soul splinter inside me, breaking into fragmented pieces, leaving a scar I was sure I could never remove.

"Julia," he whispered so softly, his breaths held out and ragged, the sound like raking gravel by hand. "What are you thinking about, sweetheart? You've been so quiet all day long, hun."

His slight movement had caused the plastic nosepiece he was wearing to fall down and I readjusted it, placing it behind one side of his ear, and then the other with careful ease. His left ear, I noticed with anguish, had begun to rot away like the bark of an ancient Southern oak tree. I couldn't stand to see it, but I pretended that everything was fine, knowing it would crush him if he knew. He hadn't seen a mirror in weeks; he didn't know. I didn't want him to. I looked away, feeling the splinter lodge itself in deeper, punishing me with its prick.

"Julia?" he whispered again kindly, taking my shaking hand and enveloping it in his, all bare fingers and bone. "Tears are beautiful."

The tears I tried so hard to hold back were resting openly on the brim of my eyelids. "But I'll never see you again." Now I was whispering too, exposing my heart like a whispered nighttime prayer. "I just want you to live," I cried out like a child. Granddaddy smiled weakly and tried to mask the pain it was obvious he was feeling, the awful, hardened jab of death, as he slowly answered me. "Sweetheart," he coaxed lovingly as I wiped my stinging tears, holding my hand peacefully, "I did."

He paused a moment and sat up, taking several deep breaths, inhales of hope and horror. I could tell he was trying to summon his strength to meet him halfway, with no success, the disease overcoming him like an ingested poison, rotten and ugly. It was all he could do now to stay awake from moment to moment; the morphine had taken its exhausting, fogged effect, covering him like a thick cloud of rolling darkness. "I never expected to live long without her anyways; it's hard to live without your heart," he said, provoking stinging tears to form, not bothering to wipe them away, unashamed at his love for his wife. He looked at me directly in the eyes, breaking my storied heart, because they were the only part of him that time and disease could never touch, an everlasting glimmer of daylight.

"The box," he whispered rashly, reaching towards the bedroom with impatient need. "The white one under my bed." I looked toward the mahogany bedroom door at his pressing words, then glanced back to see he was still pointing, still urging me to continue. "Okay, Granddaddy," I said, tucking the covers in around him before slowly moving towards the bedroom, feeling inexplicably anxious about what I might find.

I walked into the shadowed, haunted room and looked around with trepidation. Old, distressed photographs hung along the walls as far as the eye could see in every direction, black and white snapshots of a lifetime of cherished love. I knew them all by heart, but stopped to look at a few anyway. In the first photo, Johnny was with Elsie at an ice cream shop when they were very young, kissing the ice cream off her face, in the next, they were riding horses as teenagers along the shore and in yet another, they were laughing hysterically, their hands hitting the circular kitchen table that was in the next room over from me now. I came to the engagement picture taken underneath the Angel Oak Tree and felt my heart tighten like a set of new guitar strings and had to stop; it was too much. The room was filled with equal amounts of life and death in the same breath, shadows and phantoms of the past eerily close.

I stooped down and felt underneath the bed that Johnny and Elsie had bought when they were first married, an antique wooden canopy with a sweeping, intricate headboard. The box was sitting alone and I reached for its old-fashioned edges carefully, grasping it between my hands as if it was filled with magic.

"Here we go," I said assuredly, walking into the living room again, this time holding the box in my grasp. "I found it." Johnny smiled at me weakly as I set it down in his trembling hands, a half-grin splayed across his tired face. "Do you want me to open it for you?" I asked expectantly, but his thin fingers were already on the stained ribbon that surrounded it, unraveling the past with each purposeful tug.

As he unwrapped it, I slowly began to recognize that this was the secret box about which I had often wondered. It took only moments for the ribbon to fall freely and for his hands to retrieve the contents, illuminating memories of an entire lifetime: a faded newspaper clipping of their wedding announcement, cards and letters Elsie had given to him over the years, the scribbled, handwritten inscription from the headstone, and a locket that he now held between his trembling fingers.

"Julia, I want you to have this," he began, extending it towards me solemnly, as if it held the whole world. I looked at him with confusion and gratitude, asking him the question that would take me on the journey of my life. "Where did it come from?"

"The picture," he choked out limply, coughing up bits of phlegm. "The Angel Oak, I need it," I moved quickly, retrieving it hastily from the bedroom without knowing why.

"Here," I said, holding it where he could see it in my grasp, the sight of Elsie reviving him, momentarily allowing his soul to break free from the immense pain and bringing him back to life. "I have it." He looked at it with misty, sentimental eyes and I remembered the last time Dawson and I had been sitting here with this same picture, my tender eyes beginning to water at the thought.

"The necklace," he instructed, "Look at it, Julia." I turned the picture around gently and for the first time, saw something completely new in it. The jewelry lying around Elsie's long, smooth neck was the silver locket that I now held loosely in my other hand. I looked down at it again, the tears building as I came to grips with what it meant. "It was Elsie's?" I asked, struggling to gather myself, choking on my words, at the thought of what it meant.

Johnny began to cry then, his dark, soulful eyes crinkling at their corners and giving way to his wrinkles. "It was hers... it was my sweetheart's necklace from the moment that I told her I loved her. I gave it to her the day I asked her to marry me, under that tree. I had loved her for a long time, since we were kids, as much as I could understand it then. Every year it grew and by the time I understood how rare it was to love a woman like that, I knew I wanted to be with her forever. I told her that I loved her and that in my heart she had always been my wife." He paused, sobbing at the beauty of his own words.

"I was very poor and I couldn't afford a ring, so I gave her the locket. I'd saved money from my paycheck for months just so I could give her something nice. I knew it wasn't much, but it was all I had. She said yes and I remember putting it on her, hoping it was enough, hoping that I was enough. I wanted more than anything to give her all she ever wanted." I watched his eyes fade into the familiar past, almost as if she were right beside him, like the moon meeting the stars at the first sign of dusk. He was lost for a moment, but then found me again.

"After that she looked at me, Julia, really looked at me, like I was made of glass and she could see right into my soul, and with more love than I had ever dreamed possible said, 'Why do I need a ring when I've already got your heart?' After that moment, I never worried again and from that day on, Elsie always wore the locket." Johnny was talking to me, but staring at the photograph, smiling as much as his mouth would allow him at the woman who still held him, even now.

"You saw her wear it all the time, but probably never knew it. She always wore it on the inside of her shirt; she said it was closer to her heart that way."

He sighed a sigh so deep it seemed to set him on fire, like the smoldering of burning coal, igniting in him something so stirring only he could understand it. "There never could have been another. Even if she had died when we were young, there would have never been another. She was all I ever wanted." I held his hand as he cried and silently prayed I could brighten this moment, to be his new dawn, spreading light over the morning gloom. It was the first time that he had ever admitted aloud that she had died.

"Thank you," I soothed, clutching the necklace with my free hand, hoping to embody all that she was as I held it. "This means so much to me. I will always cherish it, just like granny did." I opened the weighted locket then, murmurs of her whispering in my heart, seeing two faded black and white pictures of the people who had changed me, and saved me, in so many ways. I closed my eyes and imagined the familiar tinkling of the keys of the piano in the background, her life sweeping over me like a song.

Johnny began speaking again, quieting the music of the night. "She would want you to have it and I do too. And Julia, about what you said before, I want you to know... you will see me again." He reassured, looking up from the thin photographic paper and turning to me again.

"You will see me whenever you look at a sidewalk and see initials carved in the stone... you'll see me whenever you look at any old acoustic guitar... when you feel the locket around your neck, tugging at your soul. I won't be here to talk to you or share with you anymore, but you will always have what we did talk about, what we did share."

"Memory will pick up where life left off. I'm a part of you now; all people are a part of everyone whose life they touch. You can never lose me, not really. I live inside," Johnny motioned to his heart, resting his hand on his chest afterward. "In here." I could tell that it took all that he had just to keep his eyes open as he raised his weary hand once more. "In here," he said, pointing weakly to his fading, puffy eyes. "You feel differently and see the world differently because of me, as I felt and saw the world differently, more beautifully, ever since I met you."

He gasped deeply for air again and I quickly turned up the oxygen machine. He looked at me with a painful ache that tore me to shreds, an ache that I knew I couldn't heal. "I'll never really be gone. I will always live inside your memory, inside your heart. No one can take those things from you."

I looked down again and saw that I was gripping the locket. "I can't let go," I whispered, my dark eyes drenched in tears that had finally come. He pushed my fingers tighter around my hand.

"Then don't," he said.

Johnny began to cough uncontrollably and I gave him a wad of tissues, wincing at the mixture of blood and mucus that I saw on them when he was finished. He handed it to me without a word, his weathered hands ice cold, and I put it in the small trashcan that had become a permanent fixture beside his bed.

"I love you," he continued, "I have since the day I met a spunky little girl with a black eye who called me an old burnt man." He winked at me, the action seeming so normal, so out of place, that it shattered my heart.

"I've always loved you, Engine," I smiled warily, longing to relive our time, not willing to give him up to death. "You saved me," I cried softly through my tears, knowing there was no way I could stop nature's course.

He smiled his old crooked smile, surrounded by the lines of time, and his eyes wrinkled at the corners just like they had the first time I saw him so many years ago. I wiped my eyes and in the blur of my vision I was almost certain I saw his old cowboy hat covering his dark black hair as he rocked on the front porch next to a lost little girl.

"Oh, Julia." His golden brown hands found my crumpled face and he touched my cheek gently, the softness soothing and inviting like a preview of Heaven. His deep brown eyes held mine just one last time, memorizing the face he would never again see. "It was you who saved me."

Then, before he could say another word, his heavy head found the soft, beckoning pillow instinctively and within seconds, he was soundly sleeping, a child soothed into sweet slumber. The only noises left in the still, unending night were my hushed, aching sobs and the steady sounds of the oxygen machine, its rhythmic beeping my solemn partner throughout the long night. When I awoke early the next morning, he was already gone.

Epilogue

33 Years Old

2020

Sidewalk

I t's been 25 years and I can still remember the pounding of my thumping heart beating loudly in my ears. It seems as if it was a lifetime ago, yet I can still feel his hot, forceful breath on me as he told me hastily it was time for our tea party. The wind is gusty and ragged this morning and its sudden jolt breaks me out of my long-ago thoughts. I hear the weathered, frayed screen door opening and look up to see Dawson coming over to join me on the white wraparound porch. His welcoming smile warms me instantly, mimicking the perfect summer morning.

"Hey baby," he says, taking a seat in the sturdy wooden rocker beside me. "What are you doing up so early?" I look at him with his messy morning hair and swollen sleepy eyes, thinking of the spindly little boy he was when we first met. I stare at him lovingly for a moment, remembering, reminiscent joy playing across my features as I take him in. Despite the lines of time and the years that have passed, he is still very much the same kid that I knew so long ago, now grown into the man who I love more than life itself.

"Remembering," I answer and he moves towards me, his arms widening and enveloping me naturally. This is not the first time we have been here, nor will it be, we know, the last. Silence covers the moment. It is comforting, restful and reassuring, the kind that two people might spend their entire lives trying to reach, but never find. I fall into him like a favorite sweater, warm and known.

"I love you, Julia," Dawson whispers softly in my ear, his breath soothingly familiar and subtly arousing at the same time. "Your past just makes me love you more, you know. You are an old soul living in a young body; you always have been." He continues gingerly, softly stroking my smooth, chocolate brown hair. "I've always been in awe of your incredible passion and complete conviction for doing what is right. You are so beautiful in so many ways, but it is your spirit that I have always been in love with above everything else."

I fold into him lovingly and his sinewy strong arms instinctively wrap around me tighter, covering me like a blanket, his banner of love over me. I can feel his sturdy muscles flexing tightly beneath where my head is laying and smell the trace of his faint, sandalwood cologne as the wind picks up again.

"I'm remembering him too." I point to Johnny's age-worn box on the table beside us. "Has it really been ten years, Dawson? Is it possible?"

He glances at the covered box, bewildered. "It seems like just yesterday when we finally went through it all." I nod shakingly, silent tears steadily growing in my eyes.

"The book," I say, intrigued, "I still can't believe that he thought to put it in there."

Dawson reaches for the ancient tattered box and pulls out the well-worn, aged copy of The Little Engine That Could that Johnny had left inside.

"Will you read the inscription?" I ask, my wearied eyes closing like a child seeking comfort, at the sound of the sweet words I had long ago memorized. "To my precious grandchildren, who I will never see, but who will see me living on in their parents. I will always love you, forever. Granddaddy."

My tears fall quietly, their familiar pattern enveloping me like a gentle springtime afternoon rainstorm. "I miss him," I whisper as Dawson's touch grazes my hand, the sensation trailing up my arm and finding a soft resting spot in my open heart.

"I do too, sweetheart. I do too," he says, his tender comfort washing over me like a wave coming into shore, a part of its long, never-ending journey. The haphazard sounds of little pattering feet and stifled giggles drift out into the still morning from inside the house.

"Emma Belle must be up," I say, my haunted eyes steadily tracing the yellow-orange sun as it takes its place in the morning sky. "I just hope," I trail off mindlessly, my stare glazing over in thought. I'm lost for a moment, then return to Dawson once again.

"What?" Dawson asks, studying me carefully, my tightened eyebrows and clenched jaw giving me away instantly.

"I just hope that she knows how much he loved her, the strength and the intensity of it. I don't know how she ever will." I feel like I might crumble into fragments as I finally speak the words aloud for the first time; words that are brought about by thoughts that have long haunted me in the early morning and late night hours of too-quiet silence.

My husband's rough, tan hands begin to outline the silhouette of my face and they softly turn my gaze away from the mounting sunrise. "She does know him, Julia," he pleads lovingly, peering intensely into my unsure eyes. "She knows because of you." My chin quivers reflexively and Dawson's mighty chest becomes my safe haven once again. "She knows," he coaxes kindly, choking up at the very sight of me, staring off brokenheartedly into a world long ago.

The worn porch door squeaks open loudly and already tall, dark-featured Emma emerges, a tiny reflection of us both. "Mommy!" she exclaims in her learned Southern drawl, "I'm up! I'm up! Can I wear my new white shorts today, pretty please with sugar on top?"

I smile knowingly at Dawson then, the wistful echoes of our child-like squeals and the rusty jungle gym surrounding us and give him a look that Emma is much too young to understand, a look that Elsie used to give Johnny.

"Yes, baby girl, you can wear whatever you want! It's a big day!" I say, wiping my wet, glistening eyes. She hops off of my lap enthusiastically and runs joyfully to the warm arms of Dawson, already a happy daddy's girl for life.

"Yay! I love school!" she squeals loudly before running adventurously back into the house and towards her room in delight. Dawson, looking back in time as he looks at me now, smiles at me again. We read one another's thoughts without speaking a word. She is growing up way too fast.

"Maybe she won't come home with a big, black eye!" Dawson teases openly, and before we know it we are both doubled over in side-splitting laughter, unable to breathe and slapping our knees, as if we are once again just kids.

Minutes later, Dawson kisses me goodbye and leaves for work, still as hard-working and noble as ever. In time, I find myself drifting aimlessly to the peaceful front porch, watching as Emma meets Alexia, Jessica's daughter, for their first day of school. Just like her mom, Alexia has vibrant, flaming red hair and sprinkles of freckles that can be spotted from where I am standing. Seeing them together makes my heart fill with bittersweet, soaring memories.

"Bye mama! I love you!" Emma calls out in the early morning light, stopping at the sidewalk's edge and shouting over her shoulder. "Bye baby! I love you too!" I call back, with just a hint of a smile playing on my lips. Emma and Alexia begin down the sidewalk together hand-in-hand, wriggling beneath their Beauty and the Beast and Strawberry Shortcake backpacks. They are filled to the brim, trailing crookedly behind them, nearly touching the ground from their weight.

Wistfully, I watch them without feeling rushed, knowing that Emma has already found her best friend, her safeguard for life, just like I had as a child. It makes me absolutely glow with happiness, a candle in my heart now lit. I think of all the years that Jessica and I have been through, of the soft place to land we have been for one another all this time, and of all the years still yet to come. I stand on the soothing porch a while longer, cradling my steaming morning cup of hot chocolate, my gaze tracing after the girls until they become only distant, fuzzy shadows of their forms.

The morning is crisp and fresh, the air in my lungs feeling as new as the dew on the ground. The live oaks are thick with Spanish moss as they catch the day's first breeze, blowing freely with the gusts of the wind. As I stand in the same neighborhood where I grew up, it feels impossible not to reflect back on my journey. It was here where blazes of life, flashes of death, soars of triumph, and blows of tragedy formed me in what seemed to be one moment.

The lessons still live on inside of me to this day, traveling and echoing amid the tattered, raw corners of my soul and finally coming to rest with the clamoring, scarred young girl inside. Yet after years of not understanding in the least, I finally realize that I could never regret even the vicious wrongs that I have suffered, the entrapping prison that was my life for so long. It brought me to Johnny and Elsie, to Dawson, to Emma, and in the end, even to knowing myself.

I think of all the splintered incidents that have led me to this very moment: of the monster and his stalking, fragmented soul, of my grandparents, their world so full of love and wonder; of the melody of swelling music, of glistening rubies and homemade, miniature rocking chairs. I even find myself laughing as I remember the stubborn little girl with the swollen, battered black eye.

I feel the old, enduring chain wrapped between my fingers subconsciously and look down at Johnny's priceless gift. "I'll never forget," I murmur, gently putting Elsie's shining locket on the inside of my shirt, where I know it will be the closest to my heart.

Life, I've learned in time, doesn't always last. Often it fractures and shatters like stained-glass, beautifully broken and irreplaceable. Of course, in the end, when time and breath steal the rest away, some things linger still. Some memories whisper in your heart forever.

I hold Elsie's locket against me like a promise, my healing spirit finally at rest. "Love goes on, even when life doesn't," I softly speak, welcoming the new dawn.

In the distant, hazy morning sky, I see a single firefly floating gently, her bright light shining against the fading darkness. I smile, knowing exactly how she feels.

Loved.

In Remembrance

To the real Johnny and Elsie, who death took too soon...
now, through these pages, you will live forever.

And to my sweet daddy, for the memories of
standing outside with you on hot summer nights,
feeling my small heart swell, as together,
we watched the fireflies dream.

Also By

Why the Willow Weeps

Why the Willow Weeps
Sneak Peek

Memory chased her through the night. The wind whistled like a whispered dream as she ran through the darkening forest. Her heavy footsteps pounded the ground, covering her legs in fresh mud, her breaths shallow and rapid as she inhaled in fear. With every step, her breathing grew quicker and quicker, her footsteps louder, and her legs moved- faster and faster and faster until the human eye almost could not keep up. Above all, the sound, growing with intensity every moment, of her wildly pounding heartbeat.

The rain poured all around her, thunder raging in every direction, the torrential storm causing branches to crash on every side. She could feel the distress rising up in her chest, trepidation threatening to overtake her in an instant. The falling tree limbs scratched and clawed at her like devils in the night who'd come to attack, yet still she moved, running as though the phantom in the wind might catch her, as though her life depended on it, maybe even her soul. She ran because she must. She ran to see him.

www.ingramcontent.com/pod-product-compliance
Lightning Source LLC
Chambersburg PA
CBHW032119170626
46808CB00006B/2020